St. Helens Libraries

Please return / renew this item by the last date shown.
Books may also be renewed by phone and Internet.

Telephone – (01744) 676954 or 677822
Email – centrallibrary@sthelens.gov.uk
Online – http://eps.sthelens.gov.uk/rooms

THEIR
CHRISTMAS
MIRACLE

THEIR CHRISTMAS MIRACLE

BARBARA WALLACE

MILLS & BOON

First published in Great Britain 2018
by Mills & Boon, an imprint of HarperCollins*Publishers*
1 London Bridge Street, London, SE1 9GF

Large Print edition 2019

© 2018 Barbara Wallace

ISBN: 978-0-263-08212-8

MIX
Paper from
responsible sources
FSC™ C007454
www.fsc.org

This book is produced from independently certified
FSC™ paper to ensure responsible forest management. For
more information visit www.harpercollins.co.uk/green.

Printed and bound in Great Britain
by CPI Group (UK) Ltd, Croydon, CR0 4YY

Life has a way of exploding sometimes, especially when you're on a deadline for a book.

Thank you to all the people who held my hand, gave me pep talks, and put up with my insanity, especially Peter, who didn't see his wife for nights on end, and my ledge buddy, Donna.

CHAPTER ONE

"ADMIT IT. WE'RE LOST."

Thomas Collier glowered at his baby brother who had been frowning and tapping the GPS screen for the past twenty minutes. "You lured me up to the Arctic, and now we're lost in a storm."

"First of all, we're in the Highlands, not the North Pole." Linus Collier offered a glower of his own. "Second, we wouldn't be this far north if you weren't so particular about your subcontractors. And third, we're not lost. The GPS froze and won't tell me if we're on the correct road."

What a surprise. They hadn't gotten a decent signal all day. "In other words, we're lost." He knew he should have hired them a driver. They wouldn't get home until New Year's at this rate.

A cold December rain pelted the windshield almost as quickly as the wipers could push it away. There was fog too, as thick as anything London could produce. There was no way they could see if they were driving in the right direction.

Thomas leaned forward and turned up the thermostat. The dampness had settled into his bones, leaving a chill that was going to take days to shake. He was cold, cranky and 100 percent needed a drink. Instead he was roaming the Scottish countryside.

"I'm going to be late for bedtime stories," he grumbled.

"Maddie will understand."

Understanding didn't make it right. "I haven't missed a bedtime in five months." Even if he did go back to work immediately after. The last thing he wanted was for his daughter to think he chose work over her. Ever. It was bad enough knowing that had been one of her mother's final thoughts. "It's important she knows she can depend on my being there for her."

A hand clapped his forearm. "She knows, Thomas."

"Does she? She's barely five years old. Six months ago she trusted her mother would be home too."

He watched the wipers moving back and forth, sweeping away the streaks of rain. Ahead, the narrow road disappeared into the black. "She still wakes up calling for Rosalind in the middle of the night, you know." Less frequently than she had in those months immediately after the accident, but often enough.

Those cries cut him to the quick. "A child shouldn't have to grow up without her mother," he said.

At least half a dozen times a day, Maddie would do something that would have him turning to share a smile, only to realize there was no one there with whom to share it.

"Did you know that the other day, she asked me to help her write to Santa and ask if he would talk to heaven about letting Rosalind visit for Christmas?"

"Yikes." Linus sucked in air through his teeth. "What did you tell her?"

"Something about Santa already knowing her wish and Rosalind being with us even though she's invisible. Wasn't my best moment."

"I'm sure you handled the moment just fine."

"Be better if I didn't have to handle the question at all," Thomas said with a sigh. If he had

stopped Rosalind from driving north that weekend. If he'd been a better husband. He could fill
the past nearly two years with ifs.

Woe is the man who tries to serve two loves.
You'd think he'd have learned from past generations that Colliers could either run the family
company or maintain a successful marriage,
but not both. They'd sold that right for two centuries worth of fiscal success and a royal warrant. Honestly, it was lucky their family had
survived for two centuries. If Rosalind were
alive, she would agree.

But she wasn't, and he'd never have the
chance to show her he'd learned his lesson.

"I think I see something," Linus said, pointing.

Up ahead a signpost took shape in the fog.
"'Lochmara, Five Miles,'" Thomas read. "Town
this far remote has to have a gas station. We
could ask for directions."

"Doesn't look like we have to drive that far.
Look." The road had taken a sharp turn, and
there was a building ahead with floodlights lining the parking lot. As they drew closer, they
saw a wooden sign that read McKringle's Pub
swinging in the wind.

"Who on earth would build a pub all the way out here? There isn't a soul around," Thomas noted. The parking lot was empty except for a bright red truck.

"Does it matter? They're open. We can get directions and something to eat. I'm starving."

"You're always starving."

"Because my brother insists on working through the day without a break."

Thomas sighed. Might as well let Linus have his dinner. It was already too late to make story time. If the building had any decent kind of reception, he could call Maddie and say goodnight over the phone.

If the place had a phone. The outside looked like an ancient icehouse, left over from some old estate. Its gray façade looked bleak and cold. Other than the parking lot, the only light came from slivers peeking through the shuttered windows.

"Looks promising," Thomas said.

"Stop being irritable. It's a pub, which means it serves food, and, at this point, I'm hungry enough to eat a giant serving of haggis."

"Now, that I'd like to see."

At least the front door looked freshly painted,

the red brighter and glossier than the shutters. On it hung a giant wreath adorned with tiny Scottish flags.

"Probably from Saint Andrew's Day," Linus said.

No surprise there. Considering Scotland's patron saint began as a fisherman, Thomas imagined the small coastal villages took great pride in marking the celebration of Scottish heritage. He pulled the front handle, opening the door and releasing a blade of bright light.

"Ha!" Linus replied.

Thomas stepped inside and felt his heart seize up.

The restaurant was a little slice of home. Candlelight danced from tea lights around the room, and soft holiday music floated through the air. To the left of the entrance, in what looked like the main dining room, there was a roaring fire. Seeing the greenery placed along the mantle, Thomas ached with memories of branches strewn across another mantle and a brunette curled up in an overstuffed chair.

The setting was too similar. Too much. No way could he stay there without losing his mind.

He was about to tell Linus when a man emerged from the back shadows of the bar.

"Welcome to McKringle's," the man greeted in a booming brogue. "I'm Christopher McKringle."

A barrel-chested man with a bulbous nose and neatly trimmed beard, he clapped both their backs with a beefy hand as if greeting a pair of old friends.

"Collier, eh?" he said upon introduction. "Like the soap."

"Um, exactly," Thomas replied.

It was a frequent remark whenever someone heard their name, Collier's Soap once having been a royal favorite. Usually he would go on to make some kind of proud confirmation, but he was distracted. McKringle looked like such a down-to-earth sort with his flannel shirt and wool fisherman's sweater. How could he rob the man of the only business they would probably have that night?

"My wife, Jessica, has always been partial to their lemon soap. Claims it washes away the fishy smell better than any other," McKringle said. "As you can see, we're just open, so go ahead and take a seat anywhere you like. Our waitress, Maddie, will be out to take your order in just a moment."

"You all right?" Linus asked, taking Thomas's coat for him. "Usually you wax on for a good two or three minutes about the company's heritage."

"I— I'm fine. The place reminds me... Never mind." He was being foolish. The more he looked around, the more he realized the restaurant looked nothing like the cottage in Cumbria. His melancholy was playing tricks with his imagination. "Did our host really say his name was Chris McKringle?"

"Yeah," Linus replied, settling into one of the thick oak chairs by the fire. "Maybe we're at the North Pole after all. Although, if we are, Mrs Claus knows how to make more than cookies. Check out this menu."

"After I check in with Maddie." The screen on his phone indicated zero service. "Dammit. What is it about this place and decent cellular service?"

"Will you relax? Maddie's in good hands. Nothing's going to happen."

"If I'm going to miss stories, the least I can

do is call and wish her good-night. And, no, I'm not being obsessive."

"Didn't say you were."

"No, but I could hear you thinking it." It was probably the stone walls blocking what little signal existed. "I also wanted to see if Mohammed got back with those revised production figures. If we're going to use your soap factory, we need to know exactly what kind of numbers they can anticipate."

That was the final piece of his crankiness. Literally everything was riding on this new organic line. If it failed, Collier's as Britain knew it would cease to exist.

Thinking if he stared at his phone enough he might force a signal, Thomas pushed to his feet. There had to be some way he could get better reception. "I'm going to see if the signal is stronger by the window. If the waitress comes, order me a—"

"Can I get you lads something to drink?"

Thomas's breath caught. It happened every so often. He'd catch the hint of an inflection or the turn of a head, and his mind would trip up. This time, it was the waitress's sharp northern twang that sounded uncannily familiar. He looked up, expecting reality to slap him back to his senses the way it had with his cottage memories. Instead…

He dropped the phone.

What the…?

His eyes darted to Linus. His brother's pale expression mirrored how Thomas felt. Mouth agape, eyes wide. If Thomas had gone mad, then his brother had plunged down the rabbit hole with him. And mad he had to be, he thought, looking back at the waitress.

How else to explain why he was staring at the face of his dead wife?

CHAPTER TWO

"ROSIE?" THE WORD came out as a hoarse whisper; he could barely speak. Six months. Praying and searching. Mourning.

It couldn't be her.

Who else would have those brown eyes? Dark and rich, like liquid gemstones. Bee-stung lips. And the scar on the bridge of her nose. The one she always hated and that he loved because it connected the smattering of freckles.

How…? When? A million questions swirled in his head, none of which mattered. Not when a miracle was standing in front of him.

"Rosie." Wrapping her in his arms, he buried his face in the crook of her neck. She smelled of lemons and sunshine. "Rosie, Rosie, Rosie." He murmured her name against her skin.

Hands slid up his torso to grip his lapels. He moved to pull her closer, only to have her fists push him away.

He found himself staring into eyes blazing

with outrage, confusion and panic. The last one squeezed at his heart.

"Do I know you?" she asked.

Was this some kind of joke? Now he was confused. Why would she pretend? "They told us you were dead. That—that you were swept out to sea." He reached for her again, only to have her take another step back.

"I'm sorry. I don't…" She shook her head, her eyes growing moist with tears. "I don't know…" Pressing a fist to her mouth, she turned and bolted from the room.

"Rosalind!" Thomas started after her, only to have Linus grab his arm. What the hell was his brother doing? He tried to yank his arm free, but Linus had a grip of iron. His brother's fingers were dug in so tightly they were going to leave bruises. "Let me go!" he snarled. "It's Rosalind." If he lost her again…

But Linus held fast, damn him. "Calm down, Thomas. She only looks like Rosalind."

"No." Linus was wrong. It was Rosalind. He knew his wife. Why did she run? Did she hate him that much? "I have to talk with her."

Before he could try and pull free, McKringle

barreled his way over. "What's going on here?" he asked, all his earlier friendliness stripped away. "I don't know what you lads do wherever you're from, but here we don't manhandle waitresses and make them cry."

Thomas spun around on him. "And what about hiding someone's wife from him? Are they okay with that here?"

He waited as McKringle's bushy brows pulled together. "Did you say 'your wife'?"

"Rosalind Collier." Where was his phone? Looking around, he found it on the floor by his chair where he snatched it up and quickly began scrolling through its photo collection. "Here," he said, finding the photo they'd used for the missing person poster. He held the phone so McKringle could see. His hand was shaking. "She went missing this summer when her car went off a bridge near Fort William."

Wordlessly, McKringle slipped the phone from his hand and held it closer. Thomas could feel his body tensing with each second of silence. Surely, the man knew what he was talking about. Her disappearance had been all over the news, for crying out loud. They weren't so isolated out here that he couldn't have seen at least one headline.

"She had a car accident?" the man finally said.

"Yes. Her car plunged into the river." Thomas didn't have time for this. His wife was in the other room. He needed to see her. Find out what happened. How she'd ended up out here and why she was pretending he was some kind of stranger. "Please," he said. Desperation cracked his voice. "They told us she was dead. I have to talk to her. Need to know what happened. She… We have a daughter who needs her." His control was starting to slip. Six months of pain rose back to the surface in a groan.

"It's all right, lad. I think you need to sit down."

McKringle tried to lead him back to the table, but again Thomas broke from the contact. "Dammit, why is everyone trying to keep me from seeing my wife?"

"We don't know if it is Rosalind," Linus said. "I think we should hear him out."

"I promise you she's not going anywhere," McKringle said. "But there're a few things I think you ought to know. Please, Mr Collier. Take a seat. I'll get you a drink."

Thomas didn't want a drink. He wanted his wife, but he allowed himself to be led back to his chair. Something in McKringle's eyes said he needed to do as the man said.

"Let me ask you a question," the old man said once they'd all settled in their seats. "Have you ever heard of the term *dissociative fugue*?"

She couldn't stop shaking. Hunched over the bathroom sink, her fingers clutching the vanity edge for support, she could feel her legs trembling beneath her.

Rosie. He'd called her Rosie.

She'd always thought that when she met someone from her past, she would know. Instinct would kick loose whatever it was wrapping her brain in blackness and the memories would be set free. But when this man—this stranger—called her Rosie, she'd felt nothing.

Well, not completely nothing. Her heart had practically beat itself out of her chest when he hugged her. But he could have called her Jane or Susan or Philetta for all the name meant.

Maybe he had her confused with someone

else. That must be the answer. What woman could forget a man that devastatingly handsome? Those eyes, blue-gray like the northern sea. If she closed her eyes, she saw them clear as day. Surely, such an indelible couldn't be wiped from her mind.

She looked in the mirror and studied the heart-shaped face that was familiar yet foreign. Dissociative fugue, the doctor at the hospital called it. A type of amnesia brought on by trauma. All she knew was…nothing. Her mind was a void of memories older than a few months.

At first the blankness had terrified her, but lately she'd started to grow comfortable with her empty past. Until the stranger with blue-gray eyes had walked in.

There was knock on the ladies room door. "Lammie?" Chris's gentle voice sounded on the other side. "You doin' all right?"

She warmed at the tender nickname, a term Chris used because he said she was a little lost lamb. "I'm fine," she replied. "A little shaken up, is all."

Hearing his voice made her feel better. Chris

would keep her safe; he'd been keeping her safe since the day she'd stumbled into his headlights.

"Do you feel up to stepping outside? We'd like to have a chat."

By "we," she prayed he meant him and his wife, Jessica, not the stranger with the unnervingly warm embrace.

"I'll be right out," she told him.

Ignoring how badly her hands were trembling, she retied her ponytail and wiped the smudges from under her eyes. If she did have to face the stranger again, she was going to look composed, dammit. For some reason it was important he see her pulled together.

When she finally opened the door, she found Chris leaning against the bar. "Better, Lammie?" he asked in a low voice. She nodded, and he gave her an encouraging smile.

She didn't have to look to know who the other half of "we" was. The man's presence hung in the air.

"This is Thomas Collier," Chris said, "and his brother, Linus."

"Like the soap." The comment was automatic. A bottle of Collier's lemon soap sat by the sink in the restaurant's kitchen. Jessica swore by it, and she'd developed an immediate fondness herself.

"That's right. They're up from London."

She looked to her left where both men sat at a nearby table. Both men were far more subdued this time around. The stranger was perched on the edge of his seat, his lanky body resembling a coil fighting not to spring. "Mr Collier's wife, Rosalind, is missing," Chris continued. "She disappeared following a car accident. He's pretty sure she's you."

He'd called her Rosie.

Hoping that if she focused hard enough she might conjure up some spark of recognition, she took a better look at her so-called husband. When she'd first approached their table, before the craziness started, she'd thought both men attractive. Upon second take, she amended her opinion. One was attractive. Thomas Collier was handsome as sin. If they were married, she had fantastic taste. Taller and lankier than his companion, he had the kind of features that separately were nondescript but together formed an arresting picture of angles and slopes. And again, there were those eyes. She could almost imagine white caps dotting their blue-gray depths. A slow whorl of awareness unexpectedly twisted through her midsection.

Attraction aside, however, she might as well have been admiring a stranger. "I told him about your condition," Chris told her.

"And you believe him?" A moot question if ever there was one. Chris wouldn't have asked her to join them if he didn't think Collier's claims had merit.

"Think it's worth you hearing him out," Chris said. "Then you can decide for yourself."

She chewed her lip, unsure what to do. On the one hand, if this man's story turned out to be true, she'd finally have the answers she'd been seeking. On the other hand, everything she did know would be turned upside down, and while she didn't know her past, her present was a good one.

"I promise I'll behave myself," Collier said. "You have my word I won't do anything to frighten you again. Please," he added, gesturing to the seat next to him.

Damn those eyes. How could she say no when they were imploring her?

Chris's whiskers brushed her ear as he leaned

close. "No need to worry, Lammie. I'll be right over here at the bar if you need anything," he murmured, before adding in a louder voice, "Mr Collier, might I interest you in something to eat?"

"Don't have to ask me twice. I'll take a giant Scotch, as well." The other man, who she'd already noted was a younger, less arresting version of her "husband," rose to his feet. As he headed past, he stopped to offer a warm smile. "I can't believe it's really you, Rosalind. Thomas is right—it's a miracle."

"Come along, Mr Collier. Let me pour you the best double malt in the Highlands." Taking him by the elbow, Chris led the man to the far end of the bar.

Leaving the two of them alone.

Cautiously, she slipped into the seat to his right, her hands curling over the ends of the chair arms. Jessica was always complaining that the pub tables lacked sufficient leg room underneath, and now she could see why. Her knees and Collier's were close enough that if she shifted in just the right way, their knees would touch. As it was, she could feel the proximity through her jeans. She scooted her chair backward another couple of inches, and waited.

"I'm sorry about before," Collier said. "I didn't mean to frighten you. When I saw you, I couldn't…" He paused and took a deep breath. "We were told you were dead. That you had most likely drowned in the river."

River. She squeezed the chair arms as recollections of her nightmares came to mind. Flashes of pitch-black water and air being sucked from her lungs. She had to take a deep breath herself as a reminder the image wasn't real.

Even so, her voice still came out strangled and hoarse. "Chris told you about my memory?"

"He said you can't remember anything before the past four months."

"That's right. The doctors at the hospital think I suffered a traumatic event that caused my memory to shut itself off." *Traumatic event* being the term they settled on after their battery of tests failed to turn up anything else. "You said your wife was in a car accident."

"There was a bridge collapse and your car—" she noticed he was already using the second person "—was plunged into the River Lochy during a heavy storm."

Plunging into icy waters certainly qualified as traumatic and would explain her nightmares. Then again, drowning in dreams was also a well-established metaphor, or so she was pretty sure. "I had a broken collarbone," she said out loud.

"I'm surprised you didn't break more."

Again with the second person. "You seem awfully positive I'm her. Your wife, I mean."

"Because I'd know you anywhere."

The way Collier looked her in the eye, with both his voice and his expression softening, knocked her off-balance. Here she was groping around in the dark, and he was looking at her with such certainty. Like he'd found a treasure while she was still trying to figure out the map. It left her longing to see what he saw.

"You say you know, but I would be a fool to simply take you at your word." Or be misled by a pair of stormy blue eyes.

"Trust me, Rosie, the last thing I'd ever call you is a fool. I have photos." He pulled out a phone and showed her a photograph.

Of her.

If it wasn't her, it was her perfectly identical twin.

"There are more." He swiped to another photo, this time a more sophisticated version of the same woman, with her hair in a twist and wearing a stunning black gown.

"The museum fund-raiser last May," he said. "You looked beautiful in that dress."

What she looked was unhappy. Her smile didn't reach her eyes.

The next picture must have been taken the same evening, only this time her doppelganger was flanked by a woman with flaming red hair and a handsome older man with shaggy graying hair and spectacles.

"Those are your colleagues from the university. Eve Cunningham and Professor Richard Sinclair."

She couldn't help noticing the firm way the professor held his arm around her waist.

"You're not in these photos." She rubbed her forehead. A throbbing sensation started behind her eye.

"That's because I took them."

And they were on his phone. "Is there one of us together?" Anyone could get random photos from any number of sources. It would be harder, although not impossible, to fake a photo of both of them.

"A few." Seconds later, she was looking at a selfie—and a terrible one at that, with looming faces and the tops of the heads cropped off. No mistaking her face though, right down to the annoying scar across the bridge of her nose.

Unlike the other photographs, their smiles reflected in their eyes.

"We took this two springs ago, when we were in the Lake District," Thomas told her.

"Two springs ago? Nothing more recent?"

"I'm not much of a selfie taker."

That was obvious. She studied the photograph closer. "We look happy."

We. She was starting to believe him. Rosalind Collier. The name sounded strange, but had a comfortable feeling. The way a new outfit felt when it fit properly.

Thomas took back the phone and stared at the photo. "We were," he said. "Happy. You loved being at our place in Cumbria, away from the city."

Then why did his voice suddenly sound sad?

Why was he staring at the picture with a pensive expression?

"You were supposed to be in Cumbria when you had your accident," he murmured.

Oh. That was why. A wisp of a thought taunted her, hovering just out of her grasp. Something about ice or rocks, but it slipped back into the blackness before she could be certain.

She was certain of another thought however. "If I was supposed to be in the Lake District, how did I end up here, miles away? Fort William is miles away from Cumbria too. What was I doing there? It doesn't make sense."

"No one knows." He tossed the camera onto the table where it landed with a *thunk*. "Best theory I can come up with is that you were headed toward Loch Morar. You did some field work there once. You're a geologist," he added when she frowned.

"Geomorphological features." The words popped out of her mouth without her thinking. Thomas's eyes widened in response.

"Exactly," he said. "You did a paper on the glacier marks."

She slipped a step closer to accepting his tale.

As it was, the name Rosalind was already taking hold in her brain.

"What we don't understand," he said, "is how you got here. We searched for weeks and everyone was certain you'd been washed into the Atlantic. How did you end up here in the northeast corner?"

It would be nice if she could give him an answer. Who was she kidding? She wished she could give herself an answer. "I haven't a clue. First thing I remember is walking along the motorway and being very, very tired. I didn't have a clue who I was or what I was doing."

"You don't remember crossing an entire country?"

What she remembered was being terrified as she had stood on the hard shoulder shivering in the early morning dew. "I don't even remember waking up that morning," she told him. "A truck horn blared at me, and suddenly I was there." Staring at the trees in a daze. "I was filthy. Disgustingly so." Having heard she may have plunged into a river helped explain why her clothes had looked like they'd been rolled in a wet ball. "My clothes were torn, and I didn't have any identification."

"Dear God," Thomas whispered. His chair scraped along the floor as he scooted closer. She could feel his eyes on her, waiting for what she would say next.

"I didn't know what I was going to do. Fortunately, Chris happened to drive by and recognized I needed help. He took me to the hospital, who in turn sent me to another hospital in Wick where they came up with the traumatic amnesia diagnosis."

Ironic how those memories were crystal clear. From the moment she'd found herself on that road till now, everything that had happened was indelibly imprinted on her brain.

"I don't understand." Thomas looked more confused than ever, and she suspected she knew why. "If you were at the hospital, why didn't they..."

"Look into the missing persons reports?"

"Surely you knew people were looking for you. Surely your friend, Chris, knew?"

"We did."

"Then...why?"

She paused. When he heard the answer, he wasn't going to be happy.

"I asked them not to."

His eyes doubled in size. "What?"

"I didn't want to be located. Not straight away, anyway."

"For crying out—" His fist pounded the table with a bang so loud it could be heard on the other side of the room. The noise brought Chris to the end of the bar.

"Everything all right?" he asked.

"It's okay," she replied. Collier's reaction could have been worse. Having flung himself back in his seat, he was washing his hands up and down his face. When he finally lowered them, there was no hiding the angry confusion darkening his eyes.

"Why the hell not?" He spoke through a clenched jaw, clearly trying to hold his temper.

"Because I needed time. To figure out what was going on. To see if my memory came back on its own."

"I see." It was hard to decide which was more restrained, his body or his voice. Both were being held tight. "And it never occurred to you that there might be other people whose lives were affected? Who were mourning you?"

"Of course it occurred to me," she snapped. *Though maybe not as much as it should have,* she thought guiltily. "But put yourself in my shoes. I couldn't remember anything—not my name, not how I got hurt. Meanwhile, the doctors are telling me I suffered some kind of horrible trauma. For all I knew, the people I left behind were the cause of that trauma."

Thomas hissed as though slapped. "I would never..."

"I —" Know, she almost said. Even though instinct said the thought was on target, she held back. "I didn't remember you."

"You could have looked. Your disappearance was all over the news, the internet."

"Have you seen where we are? We're in the middle of nowhere. It's not as if we're in a breaking news zone. I looked for missing persons in Scotland and nothing came up. Which only made me more convinced I might be running away.

"Anyway, I asked Chris and Jessica if it would be okay for me to stay here while I got my head together, and they were kind enough to oblige. I've been living upstairs above the restaurant for the past four months."

"Four months? Dear God." Giving an anguished sigh, he dragged his fingers through his hair, leaving the slick black locks standing on end.

Guilt turned in her stomach. Maybe she should have forced herself to look harder, but the truth was she'd been scared of what she might find out about her past and about herself. When Chris found her, the single thought in her head, besides fear, had been the words *I'm sorry*. She'd carried with her a shadow of indefinable guilt that made her wonder if she'd made some kind of horrible mistake.

Now that same shadow had her wanting to run her fingers through his hair and ease his frustration.

"Linus has been dealing with the soap factory since the end of October," he muttered. "October! We could have brought you home weeks ago. Maddie could have..."

"Maddie?"

Her heart seized up. Maddie was the name she'd chosen when Chris had asked what he should call her. The name had sprung to her tongue without a second thought. It couldn't be a coincidence Collier was using the same name. "Who is Maddie?"

He turned his face and looked her in the eye.

Son of gun if she didn't hold her breath at the seriousness in his expression. "Maddie," he said, "is our daughter."

Rosalind squeaked. She had a daughter? A little girl?

Stunned, she stood up and walked to the window on the back wall, the one next to the set of deer antlers. Chris liked to tell people the giant horns were from a reindeer, but it was embellishment for business's sake. Scotland didn't have reindeer outside of Cairngorms. One of the weird facts she seemed to simply know.

She knew about reindeer but not about her own child. Might as well stomp on her heart this moment. It had never occurred to her she might have children.

Oh, sure, she would feel a pull whenever a young child came in to the restaurant, but she assumed every woman of childbearing years experienced the same yearning. She'd never dreamed there was someone out there with half her DNA.

"Would you like to see a photograph?" Thomas asked.

"Yes, please." Spinning around, she leaned against the windowsill and waited for him to come to her. In case this was a trick, she didn't want to sound too eager. Although gushing the word *please* didn't exactly exude calm.

Nor did Collier's expression exude deceit.

Rosalind's hands shook as he handed her the phone. She was beautiful. A pudgy-cheeked angel with brown bobbed hair and Collier's eyes. The photo showed her standing on a rock in a flower garden in a sunflower-print dress. Her little arms were stretched high over her head, pointing toward the sky.

"Maddie." Her fingers stroked the screen.

"I took this on her birthday last August."

Rosalind let out a gasp. She'd missed her daughter's birthday? "How...how old is she?"

"Five."

A five-year-old daughter. "I didn't know," she said, as if saying the words aloud would chase away the guilt.

What kind of mother forgets her own child? She swiped left through the photo gallery, discovering there was picture after picture of the little girl. Laughing. Posing with a stuffed dog. Feeding pigeons in the park. And then...

She found a photo of her and the girl together. Taken when neither were paying attention to the camera, they were kneeling in front of a Christmas tree. The little girl, Maddie, had a box on her lap, while she, Rosalind, was reaching around her to straighten the bow. Longing grabbed at Rosalind's chest.

"I've tried my best," she heard Collier saying, "but she misses her mother. I can only imagine what she'll do when she sees you tomorrow."

"Excuse me, when?" Rosaline let the arm holding the phone drop to her side and narrowed her eyes at him. "Are you saying you want me to go back to London with you tonight?"

His eyes widened. "Are you telling me you don't want to come home?"

"We only just met," Rosalind said. It was too soon. Granted his story was compelling, but it was still a story. "You expect me to accept what you're telling me because you have a phone full of photographs?" Photographs of her, she added silently. They terrified her, because they revealed a life about which she knew nothing.

Shaking her head, she said, "I'm not ready."

She thought about how agitated Collier got when she mentioned not wanting to find herself. It was nothing compared to the look of horror her current answer generated. Seriously, though, wouldn't she be a fool to go along without some kind of tangible proof? Besides photos, that is. After all, photographs could be manipulated.

"Do you really think I would go through the bother of manipulating photographs and then flying all the way up here just to trick you?" he said when she commented as much. "For God's sake, I thought you were dead."

So he kept saying, and if Rosalind were to base the truth solely on his reactions, there'd be no argument.

"Look at it from my point of view. You're a stranger." Her conscience winced at the pain that passed across his face. To her, he was a stranger though, and no matter how handsome and persuasive his story may be, she needed to be sensible. "You come in here out of the blue with hugs and photos and expect me to take you at your word when I can't even remember my own birthday."

"February the twenty-fourth."

"Thank you, but you're missing my point. Would you pick up and leave your safe haven based on a handful of photographs and the word of someone you just met?"

Crossing her arms, she leaned on the sill and waited for her words to sink in. She could see from the way he stepped back that her argument made sense.

"What is it you need?" he asked.

Good question. Answers to what happened to her would be a nice start. "Time," she told him. "You're moving too quickly. I know you said I've been missing for months, but I need time to wrap my head around everything you've told me." As well as she could anyway. "And I need proof. More proof I mean, beyond the photos in your phone."

"All right. I'll have a package sent to you first thing tomorrow. You get email up here, right?"

She couldn't help but chuckle. "Yes. The restaurant has an email account."

"All right, then. You want proof, proof you shall get. Anything you need if it will help bring you home."

With that, she expected to leave. Instead, he moved closer. So close that Rosalind could smell the faint scent of musk on his suit jacket.

"I still can't believe it's really you," he whispered. "I've missed you, Rosie."

He lifted his hand and she tensed thinking he was about to hug her again. The notion wasn't as off-putting as it should've been. Rosalind blamed his eyes. In the shadows, they were like midnight. A woman could get lost in eyes like that if she wasn't careful.

"Space," she managed to whisper just as his fingers were about to brush a hair from her temple. "I'm also going to need space so I can truly think."

Disappointment flashed in his eyes, but he stepped back like a gentleman. "Of course. Take all the time and space you need."

"Thank you." She let out her breath. "I appreciate your patience. Now, if you don't mind, I need to go upstairs and lie down. My head is spinning."

Once again, Thomas fought the urge to chase her as she rushed away. Patience, he reminded himself. Patience and space. He had to remember how overwhelming his news must feel to her. Hell, it was overwhelming to him.

Out of the corner of his eye, he saw Linus

strolling toward him, a glass of amber liquid in hand.

"Here. Figured you might need one," he said.

Taking the glass, Thomas took a long drink, savoring the burning sensation as the liquor went down his throat.

"McKringle went upstairs to check on Rosalind. I said I would check on you. Conversation go okay?"

"She needs more proof before she'll believe me," Thomas told him.

"Smart decision."

Yeah, it was, and, as she'd said, one he would've made himself. Once she read her history, he had no doubt Rosalind would realize he was telling the truth.

Thomas took another sip. "I can't believe it, Linus." He might as well be walking in a dream. "How many times did you talk with McDermott about his factory? And she was right down the road." Dear God... "I didn't want to stop for dinner." If not for Linus's insistence, he would never have learned that Rosie had survived. When he thought how close the miss had been, he felt sick.

"How did she get here? Her car was on

the West Coast." Linus asked. "Did she say? McKringle wouldn't answer my questions."

"She doesn't know," Thomas said. "She doesn't remember anything prior to meeting McKringle on the motorway."

That included him. Thomas wasn't sure if that was a blessing or a curse. A bit of both, he decided.

So many nights he'd lain awake blaming himself for the accident. *She wouldn't have been at the country house if I hadn't been such a muleheaded fool.*

"And now she'll be home for Christmas." He said the words out loud as much for reassurance as anything. "Maddie's going to be thrilled."

"What about you?" Linus asked.

That was a silly question. "Of course I'm happy. Don't be daft." He drained the last of his drink in one final swallow. McKringle hadn't undersold; the Scotch was superior.

"I know you're happy, Thommy-boy." Thomas winced. He loathed his childhood nickname. "Anyone who saw your face when she walked in would know."

Thomas still couldn't believe the moment was real. That an hour ago he'd been a widower, and with one blink of an eye, his family was returned. It was a dream come true.

Making Linus's question all the more strange. "If you don't mean happy my wife's alive, then what do you mean?" he asked.

His brother leaned against a table edge, bringing them eye to eye. It was rare for the youngest Collier to be serious, so the sober expression made Thomas's pulse pick up. "Are you going to tell her the entire circumstances?" he asked.

"What am I supposed to say? By the way, did I mention I was a lousy husband and that's the reason you were driving around up north in the first place?"

"You weren't a lousy—"

But Thomas held up a hand. He knew at whose feet the blame lay.

"We've only just got her back, Linus. I'm not ready to lose her again."

He looked down at his empty glass at the residual ring lining the bottom. *Brown could have so many shades to it*, he thought. *Amber like the Scotch. Grayish brown like mud. Rosalind's eyes were chocolate with flecks of gold. Darkness dappled with light.*

He'd missed those eyes.

"It's almost Christmas," he said to his brother. "Would it be so wrong to give Maddie a few weeks of family peace?"

"You're staying quiet for Maddie's sake, are you?"

"Okay, for both our sakes," Thomas replied, his cheeks hot. He should have known Linus would call him on the excuse. "Is that so wrong?"

"No." His brother shook his head. "No, it isn't."

Eventually, Rosalind would remember everything. She'd have to remember, wouldn't she? McKringle said the doctors were optimistic as to the outcome.

When she did, Thomas would be there to fill in the blanks, warts and all, including the fact she'd gone to the cottage to contemplate their marriage's future.

In the meantime, the two of them could spend the next few weeks creating new memories. Maybe, with luck, he could show Rosalind that he was willing to change. That he was willing to do whatever it took to make her and Maddie happy again.

Then, maybe, just maybe when Rosalind did

remember the past, the problems they'd had wouldn't matter.

After all, as today proved, bigger miracles had happened.

When Thomas had said he'd give her proof, he hadn't been kidding. For the next few mornings packages of documents arrived by email. There were articles. Photographs. A copy of their marriage certificate and her birth certificate. In fact, so much information arrived in such a short time, Rosalind wondered if Thomas had a team of employees working with him. Of course, she did her own research too, since she now had names to search online.

For starters Thomas Collier, she learned, was the Collier Soap Company. Part of it, at least. He became president after the death of his father, Preston. Preston had been a busy man, marrying three times and producing Thomas, his brother, Linus, and a half sister, Susan.

When she read about Thomas online, she found herself unsurprised that he was a successful executive. She'd known when she saw him in the pub that he wasn't an average man.

Interestingly, her impression had had little to do with his expensive suit and onyx cuff links.

He would look exceptional in an orange jumpsuit. It was the way he carried himself when he walked across the room. Tall and regal, the way a man who owned the room would walk.

How on earth had she managed to marry him? From what she could tell, she was the daughter of world-renowned geologists. You couldn't get more removed from Collier's world. When she asked, Thomas said they met at university. Hard to believe a man like him would have given her a second glance. But he had. She saw the wedding photos that proved it.

By the end the week, she knew enough of her life story to believe Thomas even if she still didn't remember a thing. Problem was, being trapped in that nebulous knowing-not-knowing zone was worse than not knowing anything at all. Facts and figures answered her questions, but they couldn't provide the assurance her gut needed to fully commit.

Except, that was, for Maddie. Every time she saw a photo of the little girl, her heart swelled with longing. Maybe because she hated to see such an adorable creature going without a mother. The reason why, however, didn't matter. If she went back to London with Thomas, it would be to give that little girl her mother back.

"I don't know what to do," she said to Chris and Jessica one night after the dinner rush. "How do I go back and be some man's wife when I can't remember him?"

The two of them hadn't talked again since that night. Having agreed to give her space, Thomas limited his contact to the emails accompanying his daily document delivery. While the notes were friendly and upbeat, often filled with anecdotes relating to that day's documents, she could read between the lines his eagerness to have her home. Especially when he included the words "We miss you" in the text.

"Who says you have to?" Jessica replied. "Just because you know your name and identity doesn't mean you have to immediately rush back and start living your former life. You wouldn't rush a baby into walking, would you?"

"No." Sighing, she rested her forehead against the heels of her palms. "If only I could remember him. Reading those papers is like reading a book about someone else. I know facts and dates, but I don't feel real. Does that make sense?"

"You need to give yourself time, sweetheart." Jessica reached across the table and clasped Rosalind's hand between her two pudgy ones. For a woman who spent her days working in a kitchen, her skin was soft as silk—Collier's lavender skin cream. Thomas was everywhere, Rosalind thought. "Eventually, your heart will remember."

"And if it doesn't?" What if she never remembered Thomas Collier beyond his soulful eyes and commanding presence?

"Who says you have to stay with him? You start a new life with your little girl," Jessica replied. "I know you won't have to worry about your feelings for her."

Rosalind blushed. She was already in love with the girl from her photos and, at the end of the day, was the best reason for returning to London. "She deserves to have her mother home."

But Jessica's argument stuck with her. The older woman was right. There was no reason Rosalind had to stay with Thomas if she couldn't remember him.

That gave her an idea.

"What do you mean, a 'trial visit'?"

It was a few nights later and they were walking in the village center, Thomas having shown up unannounced for a visit. Since the restaurant wasn't busy Chris gave her the evening off so they could talk. It was, Rosalind figured, as good a time as any to share her plan.

Needless to say Thomas hadn't embraced the idea with enthusiasm.

"I mean exactly what it sounds like," she replied. "I'll come to London."

"You mean home. You'll come home."

Rosalind sighed. "No, I mean London. This village is the only home I remember. Surely you can't expect me to slide back into my old life simply because you've sent me a few emails full of facts and dates?"

The way he turned away said that was exactly what he expected. Which led to other questions as to what else he expected.

In keeping with the season, the trees on the common had been wrapped in strands of blue and white lights. A patriotic illuminated forest with branches that danced and sparkled in the wind. It was romantic, magical and no doubt the reason why Rosalind was acutely aware of Thomas's shoulder moving beside her.

She looked sideways at his silhouette. He wore the same expensive clothes as before and exuded the same command and self-possession, while she wore flannel and boots. *Night and day. Top and bottom.* Hard to imagine them ever fitting together. They had though. She'd seen the marriage certificate that proved it.

"What about Maddie?" Thomas asked after a moment.

"Maddie is the reason I'm willing to go back at all." Wouldn't matter if Rosalind had a zillion doubts, the notion of that child going another day thinking she'd died was intolerable. "She needs her mother."

"You don't think I need you?"

"You're not a little girl." On the contrary, there was nothing little about him. "And, there's no guarantee you and I will be able to reconnect. I don't want to make promises I can't keep. I'd feel better going in if I knew I had the freedom to…"

"Leave."

"Yes. I mean, no. I wouldn't leave Maddie."

"Just me."

Did he have to say the words in such a flat voice? It left a guilty knot in her stomach. "The plan sounded much better in my head." Certainly less callous. She needed to remember that as far as he was concerned, she was the woman he loved. "I don't mean to imply that I'm not going to try. I'm just…"

"Scared." The softness in his voice allowed the word to wash over her with relief.

"Terrified," she replied. Trading the known for the unknown? Who wouldn't be? "I have no idea what I'm jumping into."

"So you want an end date in case things don't work out."

"More like a potential end date. A point where both of us can step back and reassess. You've got to admit it's not your run-of-the-mill situation."

"No, it definitely is not."

Rosalind let out a breath. He understood. This was the only way she could think of to maintain some control.

"How long do you envision this trial visit of yours lasting?"

"Over Christmas and New Year at least," she said. "I don't want to do anything until after the New Year. Giving Maddie a happy Christmas is my first priority."

"Mine too."

"Then we're agreed. We'll spend the next few weeks focused on our daughter and Christmas and see where things stand in January."

"That gives us three weeks." It was clear he didn't like the idea. To his credit, however, he didn't argue. Their daughter's Christmas clearly was a priority.

"Twenty-one days," she replied. "And who knows? Maybe I'll remember everything as soon as I walk through the front door, and this whole conversation will be moot." Stranger things had happened, right?

"Have you remembered anything?"

She shook her head. "No. Not really. A few of the photos felt familiar, but I think that was more wishful thinking. I'm sorry."

The ground crunched beneath their feet. "You have nothing to apologize for, Rosalind."

But she felt like she did. She felt terrible that

she couldn't remember her family and even more terrible that she wasn't bouncing with excitement over having found her way home.

"It's not like I don't want to remember. I do." Ever since he'd appeared in the restaurant, she'd been praying for the floodgates to open and erase the blankness. The only response she'd received was her heart pounding with anxiety.

"I believe you, and I'll try not to push."

"Thank you." The tension in her shoulders started to ease.

"But..."

And, tensed right back up again. Stopping beneath a large blue branch, she turned to look him straight on. Her heart was starting to race. "But what?"

"I won't push about your memory, but that doesn't mean I'm not going to try and win you over. You should know that between now and Christmas, I plan on charming the socks off you. You'll be too enamored by me to even think of leaving."

"Is that so?" She crossed her arms and did her best to sound unimpressed. Difficult since his cocksure attitude actually was impressive. And charming.

"Oh, most definitely, Mrs Collier." He upped the charm by saying the moniker with a silky-smooth lilt. "Most definitely. In fact…"

His blue eyes bore into her. Out of the corner of her eye, Rosalind saw him raise his hand making her think he planned to reach out and touch her. She held her breath.

He kept his distance. His stare didn't waver. "In fact," he repeated, "I'm going to start tonight."

CHAPTER THREE

No ONE WOULD ever accuse Thomas of giving less than 100 percent. If anything, people accused him of being overly dedicated. When he committed to something, he went all in. Right now, that something was wooing his wife. He intended to do his damnedest to win her over before the New Year. Before she recalled the cracks. Back in the beginning, he'd been a pro at grand romantic gestures. While his inner romantic might be rusty, it was still there. Somewhere.

Taking Rosalind's hand, he led her back the short walk to the town limits where McKringle's sat empty as ever. Honest to God, how the business survived was beyond him.

The restaurant owner, of course, was more than happy to help. He packed a small bag while Rosalind did her best to make him insist she stay to work. Unfortunately for her, the restaurant was nearly empty. The only customers were a pair of short, reedy gentlemen drinking beer at the bar. When the older man rushed Rosalind and Thomas out the door with a cheery smile, she looked practically panicked.

"Relax," Thomas said as they walked to his rental car. "I promise I'm not about to take you into the wilderness and chop you into little bits."

"I know that," she replied.

Could have fooled him. She looked about as excited as a serial killer victim. Seeing her reluctance stung. When had his own wife become afraid of him?

Since she forgot she was your wife, that's when.

As far as she was concerned, he was a stranger, and one prone to impetuous embraces at that. "Would it help if I promise not to wrap you in my arms either?" he asked. Much as he wanted to.

His question got the corners of her mouth to twitch, at least.

"You know, this whole trip would go a lot better if you trust me," he said once they were underway. The rental had an incredibly responsive heating system, so he bumped up the temperature, figuring a little warmth in the air might relax things.

"I'd feel better if I knew where we were going."

Ah, he'd forgotten. Rosalind preferred to control her surprises. All right, he'd tell her. "Have you ever seen the aurora borealis?"

Despite the dark interior, he could feel her stare. The northern lights were visible on most clear nights during this time of year. Every person in the village had probably seen them at least once.

"No," she drawled. "I never have."

"Good. Neither have I. We can see them together."

"You do realize I was being sarcastic."

"Really? I had no idea."

She huffed softly through her nose, the sound carrying in the dark car. "Well played."

"Thank you. I try." The heater appeared to be doing its job. "I probably should remind you that the Colliers are known for their biting wit."

"Are they?"

"Generally, it's only among the other Colliers, but considering the number of cousins, stepsiblings and half-siblings, we're still talking a sizable group."

"I'll bear that in mind." There was rustling of her nylon jacket as she shifted in her seat. Looking over, Thomas saw that she was leaning against the door and facing him. "Your family is very interesting."

"Our family," he corrected.

Whether she missed his not-so-subtle reminder or ignored him he wasn't sure. "There's a lot of information online. Far more than your files provided."

"I figured you'd do your own research."

"Had to flesh out the narrative somehow," she replied. "Were your father and grandfather really both married three times?"

"That they were. No one would ever accuse them of not being matrimonially inclined. It was the staying married part that gave them trouble. Still, they managed to blend a few families along the way."

"Explaining all the cousins, stepsiblings and half-siblings."

"Precisely."

"Do they all work for the family business?"

If only. He could have used the help these

past eighteen months. "No, that privilege fell directly to Grandfather's true heirs. Meaning my father and then me. The rest of the family scattered to the wind with the divorces." To illustrate, he waved his hand across the dash.

"Does that include your mother? She wasn't mentioned in the report you sent," she added when he glanced over.

"A clerical error. My mother died when Linus and I were little."

"I'm sorry."

"It was a long time ago," Thomas replied. Besides, if she had lived, she'd probably have left like the others. At least this way he got to claim an intact family.

"You told me that my parents were dead, as well." In the silence that followed the comment, Thomas imagined her looking down at her lap and plucking at the hem of her jacket. "I'm glad, in a way."

"You are?" What was she talking about? She'd adored her parents.

"Not that they're dead, but that they didn't have to spend the last half year thinking they'd lost their child. Bad enough I put you and our daughter through the nightmare."

"A nightmare that's over," he reminded her. "I take it you researched your family, as well."

"A little."

"Only a little?"

There was silence again. Looking over, Thomas saw she was indeed playing with her jacket. The zipper, not the hem. "There's only so much you can discover online," she said. "Mostly facts and news articles. Doesn't really give you the full picture of a person, does it?"

"But at least you have the framework," he told her. "Something for your memory to attach itself to."

"True."

She didn't seem as excited as she should. "You don't believe your memory will come back?"

"Who knows? I'm more worried..." She shook her head. "Never mind."

"If something is worrying you, tell me. Maybe I can help." He looked over. "Trust, remember?"

Something he'd done in the last few minutes must have broken through her defenses, because she gave a tiny smile. The kind meant to offer reassurance rather than express happiness. "What if I don't like what I find? Or remember?"

His chest tightened.

You opened the door, Thomas.

"Are you talking about things to do with our family?"

"More like things to do with me."

"Oh." Relieved, Thomas dismissed her question with a wave. "You don't have to worry there. I guarantee you'll like what you discover perfectly fine."

"Says you."

"Precisely, says me," he replied. "I'm your husband, and while that might not mean anything to you, I happen to have whiz-bang taste when it comes to wives."

"Whiz-bang?" she laughed. Light and lovely, the sound warmed him from the inside out.

Thomas allowed himself a moment to savor the sensation. "Won't get higher praise than that," he told her.

"I should think not. Thank you. For the compliment."

"Try fact. I wouldn't marry just anyone."

The moment was a perfect time to reach across the bucket seats and give her a reassuring touch. Thomas loosened his grip on the gear shift only to remember his promise to keep himself in check.

He settled for giving her a smile.

She smiled back, and he embraced the moment like a hug. Once upon a time, making her happy had been his greatest priority. That he could please her, even a little, after all these months was a gift.

There were only a handful of cars parked in the lot when he pulled into the point. Thomas offered up a silent thank-you. He'd feared more considering how popular nature's light show was with the tourists. Then again, it was still early. The glow wasn't usually visible until after ten.

But then, that fit his plan.

"Wait here," he told her. "I'll be back as soon as I've set up."

Rosalind watched as he disappeared from view. Presumably to stake out a viewing spot near the beach.

Or near the cliffs, if he was planning to throw her off.

He wouldn't. Strange, really. Thomas thought

she didn't trust him, but trust wasn't the issue. Not entirely. That is, she was pretty sure he wasn't a crazy person. At the same time, however, being around him sent her nerves into overdrive. Soon as he said he planned to charm her into staying, she became jittery and self-conscious. He acted as if she were someone special, and that left her off-balance.

Maybe she should tell him to forget London. They didn't have to be in the same house for their daughter. He could as easily bring Maddie to Scotland...

"Ready?" The car door opened and Thomas reappeared, the blue in his eyes aglow in the dome light. In his arms he held a blanket. "This is for you," he said as she stepped out of the car. He wrapped the thick wool around her shoulders. "Wind gets cold off the bay."

"What about you?" she asked.

"I can handle the cold. Besides, that's why God invented Chardonnay."

Using his cell phone as a flashlight, he led her away from the crowds and toward an isolated section, as it turned out, not far from the cliffs. There on a small patch of grass lay another wool blanket along with a bottle of wine and two glasses. "I figured the lights would look brighter if we sat away from the lighthouse," Thomas said.

He sat down, then patted the blanket next to him. "McKringle picked out the wine, so I have no idea if it's good or not. He seems more a whisky man."

"Chris is a connoisseur of most things," she replied. "Far as I can tell anyway." Across the water she could see the silhouette of the Orkney Islands. Black and hilly. The water was black as well, all but a stretch of white from the moon.

"Looks amazing, doesn't it?" she said. "All that darkness."

"Looks cold." Thomas handed her a glass. "This is the most northern part of the UK. When we were here last week, I told Linus to watch out for elves."

Rosalind laughed. "Why? You think Santa and his minions are popping down for a pint?"

"Why not? Can't the old man enjoy a nip now and then?"

"Of course he can. If he's a real person." And life was as simple as sitting on a lap and making a wish.

"Don't let Maddie hear you. As far as she's

concerned, Santa doesn't only exist—he can do *anything*. Including visiting Scotland for a drop of whisky." He touched his glass to hers.

"I'll be sure to keep my blasphemous thoughts to myself," Rosalind told him. Pulling her blanket tighter, she glanced in his direction. "Are you sure you're not cold? I'm happy to share if..." She let the offer drift away.

"Thank you, but I'll be fine," Thomas answered.

Good. She'd hoped that's what he'd answer. Despite the part of her wondering what it would feel like to have those strong arms wrapped around her.

"If Santa was real, what would you ask him to bring you?" she asked.

"Nothing."

"Nothing?" She found the answer hard to believe. Surely there was something he wanted. "Everyone has something on their list, even if they're as rich as Midas."

"Except I already got my Christmas wish. Right here on this beach."

There he went again, treating her like she was some kind of gift. Rosalind's face turned crimson. Ducking her head, she pretended great interest in her wineglass. How she wished she could return his sentiment the way he clearly wanted her to, but her memory remained as dark as the water before them.

"How about you?" he asked. "What would you wish for? Besides the obvious."

"The obvious is a pretty big wish. I'm not sure I could think of another. But if pressed..." She sighed. "I think I would ask for a cottage of my own. Not that I don't like my room over the restaurant, but it would be nice to have a place to call mine.

"Then again, I guess I—I mean, we—do, don't we?" she added. Thomas's body had stiffened at the mention, making her realize her wish was based on having a life on her own. "Apparently, I'm still getting used to my identity. I don't mean to be hurtful."

"You weren't," he replied. "The situation is going to take some getting used to for both of us."

Stretching out his legs, he leaned back on the blanket. Without his body to warm the space beside her, Rosalind shivered.

"Tell you what," he said. "Tonight, we won't worry about our previous lives. We'll be Thomas and Rosalind. Two people enjoying the wonders of nature and Chardonnay."

"Sounds lovely," she replied, the tension slipping from her shoulders. "I'd like that."

For the next hour or so, the two of them talked about nothing and everything. Like any proper first date. When she looked at her watch and saw that ninety minutes had flown by, she could hardly believe it.

"I can't believe we've been sitting out here in the cold for an hour and a half," she said. Other than Chris, she hadn't talked to anyone with such ease since her arrival in Lochmara.

"And we barely touched the wine," Thomas added.

Looking over, she saw he was right. Her glass sat on a nearby rock where she'd set it earlier, still three-quarters full. "Hope it wasn't too expensive a bottle. I'd hate to have wasted your money." She noted Thomas had set his glass aside, as well.

"It's only wine," he replied. "The conversation was far more interesting and well worth the expense."

"Maybe that should be a new measure of success. The amount of wine in a bottle is indirectly proportional to the noteworthiness of the conversation."

"Or the distraction of one's company," Thomas added. The smooth lilt of his voice in the dark made her toes curl. He was definitely charming; she'd give him that. "Are you— Look."

She looked over her shoulder to see a swirl of white light swaying on the horizon. Soon, the ethereal plume was joined by green and pink and together the trio moved in a rhythmic dance. Pulsing and turning to a beat made by electrical explosions.

Rosalind had seen the lights several times, but tonight the colors seemed especially bright and alive. She felt Thomas's body sit up behind her, his proximity creating a different kind of pulse in the air.

"Gorgeous, isn't it?" Thomas's breath whispered across the back of her neck. "And it's only the beginning."

The next morning, Rosalind hugged Chris and Jessica goodbye and crossed the tarmac to the Collier private jet where Thomas stood waiting.

"Welcome aboard," he greeted.

Her "husband" had gone casual for her return, the dark suit replaced by khakis and a gray sweater that accentuated his athletic leanness. *Sleek and graceful*, Rosalind thought. Like a well-toned cat. A warm sensation swirled in her stomach.

"When you said we were flying, I wasn't expecting a private plane."

"Collier's is an international company these days. Saves us from wasting time in airports." He stepped aside so she could pass, his hand brushing the small of her back as she did so. Barely even a touch, but it was the first physical contact they'd had since their awkward hug, and therefore he might as well have plastered his palm to her skin. She straightened and stepped sprightly into the cabin. Taking in the soft lighting and creamy leather recliners, her pulse kicked up another notch.

She ran her hand along a headrest. "I take it I'm supposed to be used to traveling like this?"

"Actually, you're not. You prefer driving. At least you did before..." Thankfully, he let the rest of the sentence fade off. "Flying two hours is far more efficient than our spending the whole day on the road. This way we'll be home in time to have dinner with Maddie."

At the girl's name, she looked around, anxiously. "Where is Maddie? Who is looking after her?"

"She's spending the day with Linus and my sister, Susan. I thought you and I might use the flight to talk." He motioned for her to take a seat. "Can I get you anything? Water? Tea?"

A good stiff drink? Rosalind settled herself in one of the seats and wished her nerves could settle as easily. "No, thank you. I had too many cups over breakfast. Any more and my bladder might explode. Sorry," she quickly added as her cheeks warmed.

"For what?"

"I don't know. Using gauche language." Being on a luxury jet seemed to call for more genteel behavior.

Thomas laughed. The sound was deep and throaty. "Trust me, you've used far worse. Once you dropped a rock sample on your foot and the air literally turned blue. I'm pretty sure baby trees were stunted."

"They were not," she responded automatically. An image formed in her head, but it was merely his description. "You're exaggerating."

"A little. Very little." His expression sobered. "You can relax and be yourself, Rosie."

"That might be a problem." She watched as he took a seat in the aisle across from her, far enough away that the two of them couldn't accidentally touch. Seeing his long legs stretched out in front of him, Rosalind was again reminded of a cat and envied his composure. She was a bubbling bottle of nerves. "I don't know who 'myself' is supposed to be." In many ways Rosalind Collier was as much a stranger as he was.

Thomas nodded, understanding. Or so she hoped. "I'm not expecting you to be anything. I promise."

"Thank you." Rosalind hoped he was keeping track of all his promises; they were starting to mount up. In this case, however, the promise meant a lot.

Relaxing slightly, she allowed herself to sink deeper into the chair. The cushions were made of the most supple leather she'd ever run across. In recent memory that was. Although she suspected her forgotten experiences fell short too. Her fingers practically sank into the material.

With her index finger, she traced the double stitched pattern edging her seat belt. "Does Maddie know? About me?" she asked.

A movement caught the corner of her eye. It was Thomas shaking his head. "I thought it best if I waited until you were actually in London and then surprise her."

"I see," she said, with more than a little disappointment. Reading between the lines wasn't hard to do. She wondered if she had always been able to interpret his unspoken thoughts. "Is that your way of saying you didn't want to get her hopes up in case I didn't show up?"

"Yes."

Wow, points for bluntness. Rosalind sat back. How was she supposed to argue with the answer?

"When it comes to my daughter, I don't believe in dancing around—" Thomas explained.

"Our daughter," Rosalind corrected.

"Okay, when it comes to our daughter, I don't believe in dancing around the truth. She's been hurt enough. So long as there was a chance you'd change your mind about Christmas..."

"I would never back out and hurt her like that," Rosalind told him.

Thomas was busy studying his blank telephone, turning it around and around in his hand. "Nice words. But people say a lot of things they end up taking back."

Like the promises he was making?

The captain had sealed the hatch, and they were making their way toward the runway. Looking outside at the tiny terminal, she saw Christopher and Jessica standing in the window, waving. A lump rose in Rosalind's throat. For better or worse, the life she knew at McKringle's was over, and her new life—her new old life—was beginning.

Fearing she might cry if she kept watching, she shifted in her seat. "Tell me more about Maddie," she said. Talking about their daughter would keep her mind focused on happy expectations.

Thomas shifted in his seat as well, so that he was facing her. "What do you want to know?"

"Anything. Everything. I've seen a zillion pictures, but it's hard to know a person's true personality from a photograph. Although, she looks like she has one."

"And then some. When she sets her mind to something, there's very little that can dissuade her. She once spent fifteen minutes explaining to me why she needed to have pudding before bed."

"Sounds precocious."

"Some would say annoyingly so. But she's smart. Not recognize-your-letters-early smart, but able-to-understand-complex-ideas smart."

There was no mistaking his pride. Rosalind wasn't sure which had softened more during the exchange, her heart or Thomas's face. The lines around his eyes deepened with his broadening smile. He had a breathtaking smile, she realized. It was as if his face lit up from within.

"Oh, and she's currently all about puppies," he added. "That's her latest obsession. Puppies and purple."

Closing her eyes, Rosalind tried to merge the girl from the photographs with the personality Thomas described, hoping it would stir something. The vague image of bouncing on a bed flickered in the fog, but without context she couldn't tell if it was memory or her imagination.

"Hey." A hand, warm and solid, covered her

fingers. "I thought we agreed we were going to relax."

"I know. I can't help it." The warmth from his hand was seeping up her arm, easing her frustration. Eyes still closed, she let her head fall against the headrest.

"I just wish I could remember more," she sighed. That she could remember anything. "How can a person forget a marriage and a child? I can't even remember my parents."

"Perhaps it's a blessing."

Rosalind opened her eyes. "What?"

"Nothing." The plane lurched as the wheels left the ground. He slipped his hand from hers, bringing a return to the tension. "I was sputtering nonsense."

She tucked a leg under her and sat sideways to better stare him down. "How could you possibly think my not remembering my family could be a good thing?" she challenged.

"It couldn't," he replied. "It isn't. I meant not being able to recall the bad memories like losing your parents or... I told you I was talking nonsense."

"Yes, you were. Just like those people who say 'at least they're no longer in pain' when a person dies after being sick. Of course they're not in pain, because they're gone. Who's to say they wouldn't have taken another day of pain over leaving the people they loved? What?"

He was giving her an odd look. "When your parents died, you said that the platitudes at the funeral drove you crazy. People trying to make you feel better about being orphaned at eighteen," he told her. "You said they would have been better off keeping their mouths shut."

"That sounds about right," she said with a smile. It was an emotional outburst, nothing more, but her insides thrilled all the same. Because if she reacted with the same exasperation now, it meant the core part of her hadn't been wiped away with the memories.

For the first time since her diagnosis, she felt a glimmer of hope. It flared to life in the center of her chest and spread outward, transforming her small smile into a full-on grin.

Her eyes locked with Thomas's. Amazingly, they were a new shade. Neither navy nor gray but the color of the sky right before a storm moved in, when the clouds were dark with potential.

Suddenly, a different kind of energy wound

its way through her. The warm, heavy feeling of awareness. The air in the cabin grew thicker. It too, like those storm clouds, hummed with potential.

Too much potential for Rosalind to deal with at the moment.

"I think I might like that tea after all," she whispered.

Thomas wanted to touch her. Here was his wife, for God's sake, two feet away, looking at him *like he was a man* and he couldn't touch her. Couldn't cradle her cheek in his palm and kiss her senseless. No matter how much he longed to do so. To her, he was still a friendly stranger. A man who wanted her more than she wanted him.

Where were the blasted cups? Normally, he would have an attendant on board, but he thought Rosalind would appreciate the privacy. Her return was going to create enough of a stir; he wanted to do what he could to minimize the chaos for both her and Maddie's sake. As a result, however, he was stuck navigating the galley on his own. After opening several random cabinets to no avail, he finally managed to find the supply of Darjeeling, and set about boiling the water. A tricky task at thirty-three thousand feet, but he managed. He found a bag of biscuits, as well. Orange madeleines. Rosalind's favorites. He must have ordered them in hopes she'd someday accompany him on one of his business trips.

She never did.

Distance was a funny thing, he thought as he arranged the cookies on a plate. It built up slowly, the cracks widening subtly until suddenly there's a chasm where one had never been, and you've let your wife slip away. Maybe he and Rosalind could have bridged the gap, maybe not. Thanks to the accident, they'd never know.

But at least he had a second chance.

"I raided the pantry," he said when he entered the cabin a short time later. Rosalind looked up at the announcement with such shy expectancy, he had to clench the tray handles to keep his insides from doing a somersault. "Thought we could use something sweet."

"Are those madeleines? I adore those."

"I know." If there was a hint of smugness creeping into his voice, it couldn't be helped.

"Although I swear I didn't stock them on purpose. At least not today."

"Wouldn't matter if you did. I'll eat them regardless." She stacked three of them on her napkin, before taking a fourth and biting it in half. "'S unnerving," she said, between bites.

"What is?"

"Having someone know me better than I know myself."

"I don't mean to unnerve you," Thomas replied. Setting the tray on a nearby table, Thomas added milk to both cups before handing one to her.

"Case in point," she remarked.

"Sorry. Force of habit."

"You don't have to apologize." Her eyes dropped to the contents of her cup. "This situation has to be hard for you too. Maybe harder. At least I didn't have to bury someone. As far as I know," she added cheekily.

Amnesia jokes. Nice. "Is this where I reassure you that it's all water under the bridge?"

She gasped. "I can't believe you said water under the bridge." There was laughter in her voice.

"I can't believe you made an amnesia joke."

Their eyes met for a count of three before they both started laughing. For a moment it was as though the accident never happened, and they were just another couple laughing over inside jokes.

How he'd missed her laugh. Missed making her laugh.

The moment ended with the shrill sound of his satellite phone. Thomas groaned. One of the advantages of a private plane was being exempt from the aviation communications rules of commercial flights and maintaining constant contact with the office.

He let the phone ring.

"Shouldn't you answer that?" Rosalind asked.

"A perk of being in charge is being unavailable," he replied.

"You're not worried it's important?"

Oh, it was definitely important; he had given strict orders to call only if there was a crisis. But he was trying to prove he had changed his priorities. Even if with every ring his blood pressure kicked up a notch.

"What if it's about Maddie?"

Dammit. What if it was? Shooting Rosalind

a look of apology, he snatched the phone off the receiver. "Yes?"

It was Nilay Malik, his senior vice president of international distribution. Thankfully, she knew enough not to waste time with greetings and cut straight to the chase. "Mr Ming is threatening to back out of our verbal agreement." Ja Na Ming being the owner of the largest chain of luxury spas in the Pacific Rim and the linchpin to their new products' success. "Somehow he figured out we're using his participation to leverage the European spas and wants a deeper discount."

"Any deeper and we'll be giving him the damn soap for free." Thomas pinched the bridge of his nose to prevent groaning in frustration. Ming had horrible timing.

"All right," he said, "this is what I think we should do." Eager to hang up as quickly as possible, he rattled off instructions regarding a new set of figures that he hoped would satisfy Ming.

"Impressive," Rosalind remarked when the call ended. "You do that a lot?"

"More than I want, but less than I used to." He watched to see if the comment sparked any recollection. Rosalind's expression never wavered. She merely sipped her tea thoughtfully.

"Who knew selling soap was such high finance," she said. "Then again, the plane should have clued me in. Hardly the trappings of a mom-and-pop operation."

"True. Although at its heart Collier's is and will always be a family business. For better and worse," he added, looking down. It was his turn to contemplate his teacup.

"You know," he heard her say, "you never said what you were doing up north in the first place."

"Linus wanted me to tour a soap factory he discovered."

"Do you mean the one in Caithness, near the river? Why would Collier's be interested in them?"

"We're looking for a specific type of soap manufacturer to subcontract a new product. It's a long story. You don't want to hear the details."

"Why not?"

"Because..." Thomas stopped himself. He'd stopped talking about business around Rosalind a long time ago because anything to do with Collier's eventually turned the conversation into monosyllabic terseness. As far as Rosalind had been concerned, Collier's was a rival.

"Because?" She was waiting for him to answer, her head tilted, her hair draping over her shoulder. Unlike the other day, she had her hair down and loose the way he loved. He could make out the soft streaks of dark and light that made the color so uniquely her.

"Thomas?"

"Sorry. I got lost in thought for a moment." Offering an apologetic smile, he took a sip of tea. "We're launching a new line of luxury products this spring. High-end botanicals."

"Don't you already sell a botanical line?"

"Not like this one. These are 100 percent organic, 100 percent environmentally sound, and made from the finest of ingredients. Available only through high-end spas and other luxury distributors. It's our entry into the luxury bath-and-body market."

"But you have a royal warrant. Doesn't that already make you part of that market?"

"No offense to Her Royal Highness, but she's a little older than the customers we're targeting. We're looking for the young, hip crowd with money to burn."

"Nouveau riche millennials, you mean."

Thomas chuckled. "Among others." What he didn't mention was that Collier's market share had been steadily eroding over the years—a trend his father had stubbornly refused to acknowledge in favor of blind optimism. If the company didn't find a way to reinvent itself and appeal to the next generation, Collier's would gradually fade into extinction.

"And does the soap factory fit your needs?".

"Appears to. Linus is certainly high on them, but he sees things through the eyes of a chemist. We have to run some numbers to see if they can accommodate our production needs... This is strange," he said, shaking his head.

"Why? Granted, ours is not a normal relationship right now, but surely we talked like this before?"

"Actually, when we first relocated to London, we talked about the company often, but over the last year, you'd gotten more and more involved with your own career." Among other things.

He felt a spike of jealousy, the way he did whenever he thought about those "other interests" but shook it away, along with his guilty conscience. Whatever turns their marriage took were his fault. He would bear the blame, and he would take on the responsibility of righting the course.

Hopefully he would do so before those other interests came poking around again.

CHAPTER FOUR

SHE LIVED IN a mansion. Of course she did. She'd flown to London in a private plane. Why wouldn't she live in a stately marble manor across from a park? Her eyes scaled the building to the top two floors that Thomas said held their apartment. "The family used to have an estate in Bedfordshire," he told her, "but after Grandfather's second divorce, he decided it was too costly to maintain. Hard to keep up the grounds and support two wives."

This was their idea of downscaling, then.

The driver pulled into the underground parking garage where they took the elevator to the fifth floor. "We have the fifth, sixth and terrace," Thomas told her. "Fortunately, the building entrances are pretty private, but I've alerted Security just in case."

"In case of what?" Rosalind asked.

"The press. Your disappearance made headlines. Once word gets out that you've returned home, I won't be surprised if someone tries to snag a photo or two."

Rosalind's stomach went the opposite direction of the elevator. "I hadn't thought about the press."

Truth be told, she hadn't thought about the fact that she would be newsworthy. How naïve of her. Dead woman returns home for Christmas miracle? The story would make headlines regardless of her last name.

"Don't worry. I'll do my best to protect your privacy," Thomas told her.

"Thank you." She stole a glance at his profile. Standing tall, shouldering her one small bag of belongings. He was less than a half a foot away, but the distance felt greater. Was it odd of her to want one of his long arms to squeeze her close as reassurance? She hadn't forgotten how soothing his touch had been when he'd held her hand on the plane. If she "accidentally" brushed his hand with her fingers, would he take the hint and hold it again? She could use the grounding. Did she dare?

Before she could make up her mind, the elevator doors opened to reveal a black lacquer door adorned with a giant gold-and-green wreath. "Welcome home," Thomas announced. He unlocked the door before stepping aside.

Giving her space.

Letting her control the moment.

It wasn't too late to turn around and run back to the elevator. She could disappear into the crowds. Looking to Thomas, she saw uncertainty in his smile. He was as nervous as her. Knowing she wasn't alone gave her the courage she needed.

With a gulp and a deep breath, Rosalind crossed the threshold.

Back at McKringle's, whenever she tried to imagine the past she'd lost, she'd pictured living a simple life with a cozy cottage and a postage-stamp lawn. Never did she picture a black-and-white tiled hallway crowned by an enormous crystal chandelier. The grandness of it all made her itch, like she was wearing the wrong skin.

It didn't feel right at all.

"Are you sure we're in the right place?" she asked him, absently catching her arm.

Instantly she regretted the question when she saw a shadow of a smile, half amused, half something else, flicker across Thomas's face. She'd hurt his feelings.

"The apartment is owned by Collier's. We moved in temporarily when I took over as president. It was already furnished."

That explained why the apartment didn't feel like home. It wasn't. Rosalind felt a little better. "For a moment I was afraid I'd switched personalities when I lost my memory."

"Oh, no. You made a similar comment when we moved in."

"At least I'm consistent, then." Had she hurt his feelings then too? Really, was it all that terrible, being asked to live in luxury?

Something he said struck her. "You said temporarily. Haven't we been here almost two years?"

"Our plans got sidetracked."

Of course. By her accident. If they had made plans to move, Thomas probably set them aside in favor of consistency for Maddie's sake.

The hallway stepped down into a large living room that was flanked by a spiral staircase. Above, the second floor looked down like a balcony.

In the center of the living room, a pair of teal-colored velvet sofas faced one another in front of a white brick fireplace. They were divided by a coffee table on which sat a giant urn filled with holly and fir branches. The arrangement looked like an evergreen fountain.

Propped against the urn's face was a stuffed brown puppy, head flopped to one side.

"Is Maddie home?" She looked one way, then the other. "Is she upstairs?"

"Linus and Susan are bringing her back right now. I didn't want to overwhelm you all at once. Plus, I wanted Susan to be here when I told her the good news. Her being a behavioral specialist and all…"

"Right, right." All the support they could get.

Walking over to the table, she picked up the dog.

"That's Bigsby. Surprised they got her to leave the guy behind. He's been glued to her hand for months."

Explained why the poor little fellow's head flopped. The stuffing was gone from his neck from perpetually being gripped in a tiny little hand for months.

Months. This was Maddie's security blanket. Rosalind imagined her daughter holding him tight while she slept. To keep her safe because her mother couldn't.

Her eyes grew wet. "What if she hates me?" she said.

"Hates you? Don't be silly. She's going to be ecstatic that you're home."

So Thomas kept saying. They were all assuming Maddie would be thrilled to have her mother back. "But what if she knows?"

She turned to look in his eyes. "What if she figures out that I can't remember her?" It was one thing to be drawn to a photograph; it was another to face the child in person. "Children are incredibly perceptive. They know when someone's being fake. What if I can't… don't…?"

"You mean what if you see her as a stranger, the way you do me? It's all right," he said, cutting off her protest. "It's not your fault. It's reality."

He brushed past her and stood by the fireplace with his back to her. Rosalind wondered if the position was to keep her from seeing his expression. Reality or not, her continual reminders had to hurt. As hard as he tried, he couldn't hide all his disappointment, and he was an adult capable of understanding the situation. Maddie was a little girl.

Joining him, she stopped a breath shy of his shoulder. "I don't want to hurt her any more than I already have," she said.

"Neither do I," he replied. "If I thought that was the case, I wouldn't let you near her."

For the first time, Rosalind noticed the photo frames on the mantle. Thomas reached for one and handed it to her. It was of her and Maddie as a toddler, sitting together in an overstuffed chair. They were reading a picture book about a rabbit.

"Call me insane, but my gut says that the kind of bond you two had can't be erased like memory," he said.

"Why not? I forgot you." There she went again, pouring salt on the wound.

"Different case."

"How so?" From what she could see, he was immensely memorable. His eyes had been dogging her thoughts all week. "You're my husband. Don't we have a bond, as well?"

"Sure but, you didn't carry me in your belly for nine months."

He took the frame and set it back in its place. "I know you're worried, but I assure you, the last think I would do is throw you—or Maddie—

to the wolves. I plan to talk with Maddie *before* she sees you. I've met with a therapist, and she gave me some tips on how to broach the subject in a way she'll understand."

Some of the weight lifted from her shoulders. "Thank you."

"Not that you need to worry about faking your feelings too much. Our daughter is extremely adorable. You'll fall in love the moment you see her. I guarantee."

"Another promise. You're taking a big risk."

"When it comes to Maddie, there's no risk at all. Our daughter is that lovable. Just like—"

"Bigsby?" she interrupted, his sentence making her nervous.

Thomas nodded. "Exactly. Like Bigsby. Oh, before I forget. I meant to give this to you on the plane." He dug into his front pocket and pulled out an object. "You left this at the cottage."

A wedding band.

She'd wondered why her left hand was bare, but assumed she'd lost the ring during those missing weeks. "I took it off?" That didn't make sense.

"You don't like to wear jewelry when you're

doing fieldwork," he told her. "I found it on the bureau when we were collecting your belongings. May I?" He reached for her hand.

It was the contact she'd hoped for, but at the wrong time. Having him slip the ring on her finger felt too intimate, too much like a commitment she wasn't ready to make.

"I can do it." Taking the ring from him, she slipped it over her knuckle. Channel-set diamonds glittered uncomfortably from her hand. "Thank you for keeping good care of it."

"Of course," was his answer. He'd turned again, so she couldn't see his face. The avoidance was a relief, actually; she already felt horrible enough. He was trying so hard to strengthen their connection and falling short every time. If only she could remember something—anything—to mute his disappointment.

"Where is she? Where is she?" Rosalind could hear the high-pitched squeal through the closed doors. Thomas had been talking to Maddie for the past twenty minutes.

Twisting her wedding band, she paced back and forth across the Oriental rug. Any moment now, the doors would open and she would be seeing her daughter.

Please don't let me mess up, she prayed. *Please.*

"Mummy!" The doors burst open and a forty-inch force of nature flew into the room. "Mummy! You're back!"

Rosalind barely had time to prepare herself before the little girl hurled herself into her midsection. "You're home. You're home. *You're home*," she squealed.

Little arms squeezed her midriff. "I missed you, Mummy," a tiny voice murmured into her sweater.

Rosalind thought her heart might explode then and there as feelings, unfamiliar yet familiar, filled her chest. "I missed you too, sweetie." Her whisper cracked over the words.

Kneeling so they would be at eye level, she combed her fingers through Maddie's brown hair. The photos didn't do her justice. Those eyes. Those cheeks.

Thomas was right; she was precious.

"I missed you too," she repeated, more strongly this time. "I'm sorry I was gone for so long."

"Daddy said you bumped your head and got lost."

The simplified explanation made her smile, even as her eyes watered. "Something like that."

"I also told her you came home as soon as you could."

Looking over Maddie's shoulder, she saw Thomas watching the reunion with a soft wistful expression and felt a flutter in her chest. She caught his attention and mouthed, "Thank you." Thomas nodded.

Meanwhile, Maddie continued to cling for her life. Because Rosalind was kneeling, the child couldn't bury her face anymore, so she wrapped her arms around Rosalind's neck and rested her chin on her shoulder.

"Daddy and I thought you were in heaven with the angels, but I wrote to Santa and asked him if he would let you come home for Christmas," she said.

With each word, her chin dug into Rosalind's shoulder. Not minding a bit, Rosalind pulled her closer. "You did?"

Without releasing her grip, Maddie pulled

back, looked Rosalind in the eye and nodded. "Because God and Santa are friends."

She looked so serious about the matter, her deep blue eyes matching her father's, Rosalind wanted to squeeze her tight. Was it possible to fall in love at first sight? Or was Thomas right and some feelings ran deeper than memory?

"I guess now that I'm back, you'll have to ask Santa for something else for Christmas," she said.

"You can't. Santa only gives you one wish. Jaime Kensington asked for a pony and a racing car and a doll's house, but I don't think that's fair."

"Well, I think in this case, Santa might let you have a second wish," Thomas said. "You've been very good."

She pursed her lips in thought for a few seconds. "You're not going to get lost again, are you, Mummy? Do you have to go back after Christmas? Because I forgot to ask Santa to let you stay longer."

Thinking about the agreement she'd made with Thomas, Rosalind winced. "I promise I won't leave you again. You will always know where I am. Cross my heart." It was as true a promise as she could make under the circumstances and an easy one as well, much to her surprise.

"Yay!" And once again Rosalind found herself in the grips of a pint-sized bear hug. "And Santa doesn't have to bring me anything if he doesn't want to. Except maybe cookies. And a friend for Bigsby."

"Is it all right to come in?"

Linus appeared in the open doorway. Next to him stood a shorter woman with a mass of curly hair. Their sister, Susan, Rosalind presumed.

"Sorry to interrupt the reunion. We promise we aren't going to stay long," Susan said, coming into the room. "I just wanted to say welcome back. I still can't quite believe you're here in front of us."

Whereas Linus had greeted her with warmth, Susan's greeting was far less effusive. She gave Rosalind a quick kiss on the cheek, before drawing back and assessing her.

"You put everyone through quite a fright these past six months. Thomas and Maddie were crushed when the authorities found your empty car," she said.

"It kills me to think that I put them through the anguish."

"I'm sure. Fortunately, you're back safe and sound. For good, I hope." Although the last line was delivered with a smile, something about it made Rosalind want to squirm. Did she know about the trial period? Was that it?

"And, with that, we are leaving. Come along, Susan. I'll take you to tea." Grabbing his sister by the hand, Linus reached out with his other to ruffle Maddie's hair. "Have fun with Mummy, Maddie-cakes. Oh and, Thomas, turn your phone back on. I've been fielding panic calls from the office for the last hour."

Thomas sighed. "What now?"

"Let's just say Legal's involved and leave it at that," his brother said. He continued dragging Susan toward the door. "Goodbye again, Rosalind. We're glad you're home."

Rosalind watched the two them depart, then turned to Thomas, whose expression had darkened slightly.

"What does that mean? Legal's involved?" she asked.

"Nothing good. Never is when lawyers are involved." Taking Rosalind's elbow, Thomas helped her to her feet while Maddie continued to hold fast, and led them to one of the sofas.

"No, I suppose it isn't." She frowned. "Were there problems between your sister and me?"

"What do you mean?"

"The way she spoke. If I didn't know better, I'd say she was angry with me."

"That's just Susan being Susan. She doesn't do big emotional scenes very well. How are you doing, sweet pea?" He tweaked Maddie's nose. "Happy Mummy's home for Christmas?"

"Uh-huh. Can we put up the Christmas tree now? And decorate it? And put candles in the windows?"

"Whoa, easy does it. Your mummy just got home. There's plenty of time before Christmas yet."

Conversation nicely deflected. She made a note to probe deeper later on. At the moment, she wanted to focus on Maddie who, despite Thomas's admonishment, not only wanted the tree decorated and stocked with presents, but three different types of Christmas pastries baked.

"We don't even have a tree," she pointed out. "Shouldn't that be the first step?"

"We could get one tonight," Maddie replied. "I saw them when Uncle Linus took me to see the Gingerbread City. You said I could put the angel on top this year. And can we have snowflakes?"

Her enthusiasm had Rosalind exhausted, and they hadn't yet started. She could see what Thomas meant about her being persistent.

"What do you think?" she asked Thomas. She needed him to help slow Maddie down. However, he was reading something on his phone and didn't hear her.

"Thomas?"

"Sorry," he said, looking up. "Legal buzzed with a text."

Of course they did.

The caustic thought popped into her head unbidden. Where did it come from? And why did it leave her agitated?

"Tell you what," Thomas said to Maddie. "How about if I call and make arrangements for a tree to be delivered tomorrow? The three of us can decorate it tomorrow night. That will give Mummy time to catch up on everything she's missed while she was gone."

"Did you forget where your room is? I can show you," Maddie offered.

"I'd rather see your room," Rosalind said. "Daddy told me it's a new color."

"Purple! Daddy and Uncle Linus painted it. I wanted purple curtains too, but Daddy hired some lady who made them with orange flowers instead." The little girl rambled on about Linus getting purple paint in his hair.

"Wow. Sounds like Uncle Linus isn't much of a handyman." She looked to Thomas expecting a response, but he was again reading his phone. "If you need to call them back..." she said, checking the sigh that rose with her words.

To say Thomas looked apologetic was an understatement. "It'll only take a second, I promise."

Right. Again, the thought was unbidden. This was obviously not the first time these thoughts had plagued her.

"Don't be sad, Mummy."

Shaking her thoughts away, Rosalind smiled at Maddie. "Why would I be sad? I'm back home with my favorite little munchkin."

"About Daddy working. He doesn't do that anymore."

"He doesn't?"

"He used to work all the time, but then you got lost and now he doesn't." Maddie jumped off the sofa and held out a hand. "Come on, Mummy. Let's go and see my room."

But as they headed upstairs, Maddie chatting a mile a minute, Rosalind couldn't shake the feeling of agitation in the pit of her stomach. The annoyed reactions, his sister's coolness, the missing wedding band. Why did she get the feeling there was a piece to her history that Thomas wasn't sharing?

It was close to midnight when Thomas dragged himself back to the apartment. Nights like this were exhausting, especially when he'd much rather be home with Rosalind and Maddie, but he was committed to securing Collier's future. It was his family's legacy. His daughter's legacy. And, he'd be damned if he was going to be the Collier who led the company to ruin. If he could just get this botanical line launched. It was the first project he'd created from concept to product, the first Collier's product where he was the Collier in charge, and everything rode on its success.

Rosalind never understood…

No. He shook away the thought. He was the one who'd messed up, not Rosalind. This time would be different. He'd show her.

He just needed to get through this launch.

The house was dark as he made his way upstairs. Checking in Maddie's room, he found her in bed, arms flung akimbo in a deep, carefree sleep. He retrieved Bigsby from the floor and propped the dog next to her pillow before kissing her good-night and closing the door. By habit, he walked straight across the hall to his room, his hand just about on the handle when he remembered. Rosalind was in there. He'd relegated himself to the spare room for the unforeseeable future. Out of respect for her condition.

He nearly groaned. How respectful was he now with his body aching to peer inside? For six long months, there'd been nothing but emptiness on her side of the bed. He longed to feel the warmth of her body pressed tight against his.

Soon. He meant what he'd told her. He would

do everything in his power to convince her she should stay past the holidays. It would be the best Christmas present he could ever ask for.

He went down the hall to his room.

At first, when he heard the noise, he thought it was Maddie having one of her bad dreams. Half stumbling, half hopping into his pajamas, he headed to her room only to realize the noise came from the master bedroom. Rosalind was the one having the nightmare. Through the heavy door, he could hear her moaning.

Without giving it a second thought, he rushed inside to find Rosalind fighting the covers, her legs thrashing about and getting tangled in the thick duvet. Just as he did when Maddie had her dreams, Thomas sat on the mattress's edge and stroked the hair from her face.

"Shh," he whispered, making sure to keep his voice soft and gentle. "Everything's all right." With his free hand, he pulled the covers away from her flailing limbs. Freed from the tangles, Rosalind's arm swung wide, smacking him on the side of the head.

Oof! He grabbed her wrist to keep her from hitting him again, then curled his other hand behind her head. "Wake up, sweetheart. You're having a bad dream."

As he spoke, he lifted her into a sitting position until her cheek rested against his shoulder. She was gasping for breath, so he let his hand slide from her neck to her spine, gently stroking up and down until he felt her breathing calm.

An arm slipped around his arm to grip his shoulder.

"That's right," he whispered. "You're safe."

"I... I..." Rosalind lifted her head. Thomas could feel the air from her parted lips hitting his. "What...?"

"You were having a nightmare," he repeated.

He wished he hadn't spoken. As soon as she heard his voice, she tore from his grip, hitching backward until she was pressed against the headboard. Thomas swallowed back the punch her panic sent to his gut.

"You were yelling. I heard you crying out through the wall."

"I was..."

The light from the hallway leaking into the room was just enough that he could see her eyes fall to his bare chest. The man in him took pleasure in her awareness. Lord knows he was painfully aware of her bare legs.

"I was underwater," she said after a pause, "and I couldn't breathe. I kept trying to get my head above the surface, but I was stuck. There was something holding me in place. I think it was a seat belt."

The hair on Thomas's arms started to stand up. "You were dreaming about the accident?"

"I don't know. Maybe. All I know is I was sure I was going to die. Then I heard your voice and…" She combed the hair from her face with her fingers. "Could I have some water?"

"Or course." Reluctant as he was to pull away, he walked to the bathroom. When he came back, she was sitting propped by a pillow with the covers pulled up once more.

"Could you really hear me through the walls?" she asked as he handed her the glass.

"Thought it was Maddie at first, having one of hers."

"Maddie has nightmares?"

"Every now and then. I suspect they'll be better now that you're back."

"I caused her nightmares."

The guilt in her voice stung him. "She missed

her mother. It's not your fault. You didn't have an accident and wander Scotland with amnesia on purpose."

"If I did, then we're talking even bigger problems."

"Yes, we are."

Taking the cup from her hand, Thomas placed it on the nightstand. She looked pale and shaky in the dim light. The vulnerability of it all struck him hard. Without thinking twice, he was on the edge of the bed again, brushing her cheek with the back of his hand. "Feeling better?" he asked. She nodded, and his nerves relaxed a little. "Good. Then let's finish tucking you in."

He waited until she lay down before pulling the covers to her chest and molding them to her sides. Same way he did when Maddie needed tucking in.

Though in his mind, he wasn't thinking about Maddie. He was seeing Rosalind's cotton T-shirt and thinking about the long legs exposed below.

I never did like fancy lingerie.

"What's the point if you're sleeping?"

Thomas ducked his head, unaware he'd spoken his thoughts aloud. "So you always used to say."

The air turned awkward as they both fell silent. He should move, thought Thomas. Stand up and let her return to sleep. Instead, he sat on the edge of the mattress with his hands resting on either side of her arms. The closest thing to an embrace he could have.

"Thank you for the water," Rosalind said. "And for coming to my rescue."

"Anytime." He was sorry he'd failed her to the point she'd ended up having nightmares in the first place.

"You must be tired. What time is it, anyway?"

"A little after two, and don't worry. I'm used to not getting a lot of sleep."

"You work late a lot."

Something shifted and Thomas felt a tension that wasn't there before. His guilty conscience, he supposed. "Only in cases of emergencies these days, I promise." Unfortunately, this launch threatened to have a lot of emergencies. "I'm sorry I ruined your homecoming."

"It's all right."

"No, it's not. You deserve special. Besides, I

promised you that I would be so charming and debonair that you'd forget all about this trial visit idea of yours."

"Forget?" She gave a soft snort.

"*Discard* then," he replied with a grin. Discard, forget, toss aside. All of those. "I promise that tomorrow I will make everything up to you. We're talking full-on charm offensive."

"Sounds more like a battle than a homecoming."

"Well, you did issue a challenge back in Lochmara, and I never—" he leaned in for emphasis "—back down from a challenge. You won't be able to resist."

With that, he dipped his head, not too far but enough that he heard her breath hitch in expectation. It was a noise he hadn't heard in a long time, and damn if he hadn't missed it down to his core.

If she wasn't in a vulnerable place and if he weren't such a gentleman…

"I'll let you get some sleep," he whispered.

Indulging himself in one more feathery brush of her cheek, he rose and headed to the door.

"Thomas?" Her voice called out as he reached the door. "Would you mind…?"

Closing the door tight behind him? He waited for the command. "What do you need?"

"Never mind. I don't want to put you out."

"Don't be silly. If you need something, all you have to do is ask."

She looked down at her lap, her hands fidgeting atop the duvet. "I was wondering if you wouldn't mind sitting with me a little longer. Just until I fall asleep."

Sit. Her choice of words was obvious as she pointed to the wingback chair in the corner by the armoire. Still, he wasn't one to refuse the opportunity. Pulling the chair closer to what was normally his side of the bed, he sat down with one foot perched on the mattress. "Have you had a lot of nightmares? Since the accident?"

"Back when Christopher found me and I was in the hospital, I had them, but this is the first time in a long time. And it's the first time I've dreamt with such detail. Before they were more vague and foggy."

"That's a good sign. Maybe you're starting to remember."

"Or I looked at too many accident scene photos," she replied.

"You don't believe that's the case though, do you?" He recognized downplaying when he heard it. She was afraid to be too hopeful.

"It seemed so real. I could feel the water closing in on me and the steering wheel…"

Thomas heard the rustling of sheets as she kicked her legs again. Instantly, he put his hand on her knee to stop her from moving. "You're trembling."

"Like I said, the dream was very real."

Forget keeping his distance. He stretched out atop the duvet and pulled her to his side before she could utter a protest. That she went so willingly spoke volumes.

"Luckily for you, there's no water within miles of this bedroom, unless you count the fountain in the park, and I don't think that's in danger of overflowing all the way to the sixth floor. Certainly be interesting if it did though."

She capitulated without argument when he urged her head to his shoulder, sending a surge of pleasure through him. Not sexual pleasure, but happiness that she trusted him. Who knows? Tomorrow they could be back to being awkward around each other, but for now the distance had been breached. A little, anyway.

"Can you imagine? Boats sailing down St. James's Street? Be a sight, wouldn't it?" He combed her hair with his fingers. Slow, methodical strokes aimed at soothing the tremors from her body. Little by little, her muscles began to relax, her breath becoming deeper and slower.

"Tell me something," she murmured, her breath ghosting across his bare chest. "About us."

"Should I tell you about the first time we went hiking? It was right after we met and we decided to climb Cat Bells. Proper city boy that I was, I'd never done much hiking, but I didn't want you to know that. So a couple days before we left for the weekend, I went out and bought brand-new hiking gear. Then I drove over the stuff with my car a couple times to make it look used."

"Your car?" she slurred.

"A couple of pints may have been involved in creating the idea. Anyway, the day of the hike there I was in my brand-new, completely trashed hiking gear all set to impress you and..."

He paused. Rosalind's breath had evened out.

Closing his eyes, he concentrated on the sound of his heart beneath Rosalind's cheek. "I got the biggest blisters you've ever seen that weekend, but I didn't say a word," he whispered. "Because you were having the time of your life. I'd do anything to win that smile."

He pressed a lingering kiss to the top of her head. "If it's the last thing I do, I'm going to earn that smile again."

CHAPTER FIVE

ROSALIND WOKE TO an empty bed and a strangely disappointed heart. The latter surprised her. She hadn't asked, or wanted, Thomas to spend the night.

She hadn't asked him to hold her until she fell asleep either, but he did, and Lord help her, she'd liked it.

Or was it simply the comforting shoulder she appreciated? Last night's dream was still in her head. The water rushing around her midsection. The searing pain in her shoulder. The shattering of glass as she smashed…something hard. Against the cracked windshield.

She winced as pain stabbed behind her right eyeball. Maybe it was a memory.

Pinching the bridge of her nose, she closed her eyes and concentrated on better thoughts. Like the rhythm of Thomas's fingers combing her hair. Last night was the safest she'd felt in a long time, an absolutely terrifying thought.

How could she feel safe and secure yet still not remember the man?

And then there was the inexplicable annoyance rising up inside her when it came to his business. It was understandable she would find his distraction on her first day home frustrating. But her response felt deeper and almost bitter. Why?

She'd get no answers lying in bed. Where was her bag? Looking around, she spied it by the armoire, open and emptied. Meaning someone had unpacked her things.

She was officially moved in. Rosalind waited to let the realization sink in.

The clothes she'd brought weren't much. A handful of sweaters and jeans Jessica and Chris had bought for her and a few more she'd bought with her wages. They hung in the armoire with other clothes. Her clothes, Rosalind corrected. She trailed her fingers across the hangers. Like everything in the house, the outfits were familiar and new. A copper sweater caught her eye. It was long and airy, the yarn impossibly soft. A voice in her head said wearing it would be like wearing a hug.

She could use a hug. She grabbed the sweater

from the hanger, only to squeeze the fabric in her fist as images flashed behind her eyes.

A tree. White lights twinkling in the snow. An arm in a copper-colored sweater reaching around her waist.

"Will you still want to hug me when I'm as big as a house?"

"Always."

Thomas's breath, warm as he buried his face in the crook of her neck and rained tiny kisses above her collar.

"Always," he whispered again.

Rosalind sighed.

The hanger clattered to the floor, and the images disappeared. She was left in her room with nothing but a bunched-up sweater in her hand.

And a tingling sensation lingering on her neck.

It was clearly a memory. As soon as she finished dressing, Rosalind rushed to find Thomas so she could ask him to add context to the moment playing in her head.

She found him heading up the spiral staircase. Actually, they collided. She pitched into his chest, her hands grabbing on to his shoulders for balance while his ars wrapped around her waist. Smelling the traces of musk and wood on his shirt, she immediately traded the morning's memory for one from the night before. When he'd held her against his bare skin until her nightmare abated. He'd smelled so delicious her body had wanted to melt into the scent.

"Careful there," he said. "Don't need you taking a header over the railing. Everything all right?"

His grip tightened. "You didn't have another nightmare, did you?"

"What?" Rosalind shook herself from her thoughts. Hopefully, he would think the rush the reason for her red cheeks.

"No. Nothing like that," she replied. "Slept like a baby." Thanks to him, but she didn't say that. She hadn't had a chance to process how safe and protected she'd felt in his presence or what those responses meant to her.

"I'm glad to hear. You're up pretty early. Maddie doesn't wake for another hour or so."

"Actually..." She lifted her eyes to his, struck for the umpteenth time over how the blue changed shade depending upon the circumstances. Like right now they were a mix of blue and gray. "I was looking for you."

"You were? Do you need something?"

"Yes, I..." His gaze had lowered to her lips, causing her pulse to stutter and calling attention to the fact they were still wrapped in an embrace. Removing a hand from his shoulder, she pointed to the living room below. "Do you think we can take this downstairs?"

"Certainly." The tiniest bit of red dotted his cheeks as he released her and took a step backward. Rosalind grabbed hold of the railing. She hadn't expected to feel off-balance.

"There's fresh coffee in the dining room. Why don't I pour us a cup and join you on the sofa?"

Giving her a moment to recover. "Wonderful," she said.

"Do you still take it with milk and no sugar?" he called out just as she was stepping off the bottom step.

"You mean you forgot?"

"Not really, but I thought I'd ask so you wouldn't feel like you were at a disadvantage."

Like yesterday with the tea and cookies. She had called the experience unnerving. Considering the entire world probably knew more about her than she did, pretending not to know her coffee preference was a pretty minute gesture. Nonetheless, she warmed from the inside out.

"I bet I could guess yours," she said.

Thomas came walking in carrying a pair of bone china cups and saucers with gold rims. He stopped short of the coffee table and raised the cup a little higher, so she couldn't look at the contents. "You think so, do you? Let's give it a go then."

She looked him up and down. He'd returned to corporate mode albeit without a jacket. His white dress shirt was crisp and perfectly tailored to show off his upper body. His cuff links were simple onyx circles. Elegant and understated. With just the right amount of style, she added, taking in his brightly striped tie. The man was clearly made for sophistication. And to be in command.

"Black, one sugar," she said. Simple with just a touch of sweetness.

Thomas's eyes widened. "Was that really a guess or did you remember?"

"Lucky guess." Although given how the answer had popped into her head with such certainty, maybe luck wasn't as involved as she thought.

She took a sip of coffee and let the caffeine enter her system. The house was quiet, and she took advantage of the silence to catch her breath.

"Speaking of—"

"I have a present for you."

They spoke simultaneously. "You first," she said. "Presents before conversation."

"Sounds like a child I know." Thomas reached into his pocket and pulled out a phone.

"We were fortunate to get the same number," he said. "I had my assistant recreate as many of your contacts as possible, although I'm sure there are a few he missed. Eve from the university is in there though. Sinclair, as well."

Those were the people from the photo he'd showed her the night he found her. Apparently, Thomas wasn't a fan of the gentleman.

"We're working on getting your license, as well."

Rosalind turned the phone round and round in her hand. What would happen if she were to call one of her contacts right now? What would they say? Would they think her a prank caller?

"Do any of them know I'm back?" He'd said yesterday he was trying to preserve her privacy.

"Not yet." He paused to drink his coffee in what looked like a well-crafted delay tactic to gather his thoughts. "I was going to ask our lawyers to make an announcement today—that is, with your permission."

The world would have to be told sooner or later. Much as she'd like to simply resume her life, too much time had passed. "Would I have to talk with the press?"

"You don't have to do anything you don't want to," he told her. "There may be a few reporters trying to snag photos, but we'll do our best to keep them away. The good thing is that while our name is famous, we're not on a par with the Royal Family. Most of London wouldn't recognize a Collier even if they walked right into us."

"Is that your way of telling me people won't be gawking when I cross the street?"

"Precisely. You could walk out of the apartment this morning and no one would be the wiser as to who you were, unless you wore a sign around your neck."

"Thank goodness for anonymity," she said, still staring at the call screen.

"It does have its moments." Thomas took her hand. "Hey—you're in control. Fast, slow. However you want to return to the world is up to you. If you want to stay locked up in the apartment until Christmas, that's fine with me. It's your call."

Again, his kindness warmed her, even if it wasn't entirely practical. "I can hardly spend the entire month hiding from the world. Sooner or later I'll have to show my face."

Which reminded her. "You've mentioned the university several times now. Do I work there?" It occurred to her that returning to work might be a good way to ease herself back into the world. Give her something outside of herself on which she could focus.

"You...used to." Thomas pulled his hand away. "Your research lost its funding, and you were let go."

"Oh." So much for that idea.

"I'm sorry."

"Why are you apologizing? It's not your fault." The apology, she suspected, was in re- action to the disappointment on her face. She hadn't expected to feel that let down. "So no research. Do I work anywhere?"

Thomas shook his head. "Losing your funding left you at loose ends. You wanted to work but were struggling to find a new research project you felt passionate about. In the meantime, you were staying home with Maddie."

"I bet that made her very happy."

"Maddie? Deliriously so."

Something felt missing from his answer. Rosalind sensed incompletion. She sipped her coffee and waited to see if he'd take advantage of the silence to continue.

Instead, he pivoted the conversation. "Your turn," he said. "Why were you looking for me?"

Right! The whole reason for her excitement. "Something very strange happened to me upstairs."

"What do you mean, 'something happened'?" He scooted closer so their knees were touching. "You said everything was all right."

"Everything is fine. Except that when I was getting dressed I had a… Well, I guess you could say I had a memory come back to me."

"Are you sure? What kind of memory?"

"I'm not sure." *Us in love.* "It came to me in a

flash." She told him about the lights sparkling in the window and the tree laden with rustic ornaments.

"Mostly woolen balls and felt animals. And I was pregnant." She left out how he'd nuzzled her neck and vowed eternal devotion.

While he was smiling, a shadow passed across Thomas's blue eyes. "That was in Cumbria. In the cottage."

"The one I was visiting last June." He'd mentioned they'd lived there prior to his father's stroke. "You showed me a photo we took there on holiday. A selfie." Was that why she had pictured the cottage? Had talk of tree decorating and photographs planted ideas in her head?

Then again, their faces had filled the frame leaving very few details for her to remember. If the scene she saw upstairs was from her imagination, she had an extremely vivid one.

"We seemed very happy there," she said out loud.

"We were. You loved Cumbria."

We'll go back, I promise.

Thomas's words sounded in her head, not at the table. She looked over to where he was fiddling with his coffee cup.

"What happened?" she asked him.

"What do you mean?"

"Yesterday, you said we'd moved in here temporarily. We were planning to go back, weren't we?"

"Wow, you really are getting your memory back." He was smiling, but something about his expression felt off. His eyes weren't as bright as they were a moment before. It was as though the mention of Cumbria had dampened his excitement. "You're right. Our original plan was to go back when my father recovered."

"Except your father didn't recover."

"No," Thomas said with a long sigh. "He did not."

So, Cumbria had been postponed because of his father's death. And perhaps again because of hers?

"I'm sorry," she said. "I didn't mean to bring up a bad subject."

"You didn't." Clearing his throat, he repeated in a softer voice, "You didn't. What matters is that you're starting to remember and that is wonderful. In fact, I think this calls for a celebration." This time his face lit up contagiously.

"You're only saying that because you were

already planning to unleash a full charm offensive."

And…his smile faded.

"What?" Rosalind asked. She could guess the answer. Thomas was staring at his coffee cup like the contents would disappear if he didn't.

"I arranged to meet with the lawyers this morning so we could finish what we started last night."

Of course he did.

"I didn't expect you up this early," he said. "The idea was to get in and out of the office before you even realized I'd left."

Rosalind nodded.

"I'd only go if it was an emergency."

"I know." She was disappointed. What bothered her was how strongly her disappointment struck her. With such bitterness and anger. They'd had this conversation before.

"I promise…" Setting both of their cups on the coffee table, Thomas took her hands in his. "I'll wrap this up as soon as I can and then the charm offensive shall be unleashed. You have my word."

She was still disappointed, but she understood. His world didn't stop simply because she'd returned to it. "Fine, but there'd better be a lot of charm."

"Shock and awe. You have my word."

"Are you still here? Shouldn't you be home with your wife and daughter?"

Thomas was in no mood for his brother's cheerfulness. "Whoever invented lawyers should be hung, drawn and quartered."

"I don't think they were actually invented."

"You know what I mean," Thomas snapped. He should have gone home ages ago, but the day just wouldn't cooperate. Soon as he got one fire out, another would crop up.

He tossed his files on the conference table before throwing himself into the head chair. The chair rolled backward, stopping when it bumped into the whiteboard behind him. "Maybe I should call the whole thing off," he said to the ceiling. "Forget the new spa line. Let the company fade away. Two hundred years is a long enough run, don't you think?"

"You couldn't let Collier's fade away any more than you could cut off your head," Linus replied. "If you could, you never would have stopped playing country carpenter and come back."

A fateful decision if ever there was one. "I came back because Dad said he needed me."

"And stayed because Collier's did." Ignoring the chairs in favor of sitting on the conference table, he started straightening the papers that had spilled out of Thomas's file. "On the plus side, you're a hell of a lot better at running the place."

"Than who? Dad? He didn't exactly set the bar very high."

More like laid the bar on the ground. Whatever Preston Collier had done, it hadn't been successfully running a company. The last decade had been a fiscal disaster, and now it was up to Thomas to fix things. Linus, the coward, chose to go into science.

"I'm sorry your reunion last night didn't go as planned," Linus said. "How is Rosalind settling in?"

"About as well as you'd expect." His brother didn't need to know about Rosalind's nightmare or the fact he'd held her in his arms for most of the night while she slept. "She's remembered a few things."

"You're kidding? That's terrific. So why aren't you smiling?"

"She remembered that my return to Collier's was supposed to be temporary."

"I see." Linus stroked his chin. "Does she remember why you stayed?"

"That Dad died and I stayed on to run the company? Yes. But not how opposed she was to staying in London. Give her time though. She'll remember soon enough."

Along with remembering how unhappy she'd been about all the hours he'd worked and how neglected she'd felt. When that happened, how long would it take before they were right back to where they'd been in June? With her walking out their front door.

Groaning a second time, he let his head fall back against the chair. "I promised her we'd spend the day together."

"So why not go do that?"

"Because Ernie messed up the contracts regarding the new shampoo, and now we have to somehow retroactively retain the rights without spending an arm and a leg. That's why."

"So have Ernie and the legal team fix it. There is such a thing as delegation you know."

Thomas lifted his head. "Dad delegated."

Need he say more? Until he was certain Collier's was safely back from the brink, he had no choice but to oversee every detail. Linus was right. He'd sooner cut off his head than see Collier's fail.

Even he had his limits though. "I can't let Rosalind walk away again," he said.

"You don't know if she's going to walk away."

"I know I'll do whatever I have to in order to prevent it," Thomas replied.

Heaving the loudest sigh known to man, his brother pushed himself to a sitting position. "What if she wants you to walk away from Collier's? Can you?"

"I walked away from Collier's before. Carpenter in the woods, remember?"

"That was when you were just out of university and all starry-eyed about being in love. You hadn't actually fulfilled your destiny at that point."

"Running Collier's is hardly my destiny."

"Keep telling yourself that, Thommy-boy." Linus pushed himself off the table and onto his feet. "You were meant to run this company, and you love it. Lawyers and all."

Yeah, he did. But he loved Rosalind too. And unlike the other Colliers in history, if forced to choose, he knew the correct decision to make.

CHAPTER SIX

"I KNOW. I KNOW. I should have been home hours ago. The day started badly and went downhill from there." Thomas rushed into the apartment stripping off his coat and suit jacket as he walked. "Let me…"

Hitting the bottom step, he drew up short realizing he was speaking to an empty room.

Of course he was. Did he expect his family to be sitting on the sofa waiting for him?

That didn't stop his pulse—or his guilty conscience—from kicking up a notch. A better man would have walked out of the meetings and told Legal to hash out the problem on their own. But he wasn't a better man. He was a Collier and it was his name signed on the bottom line, so he'd stayed.

"Rosalind?" He tossed his jackets on the sofa and started working on the tie. "Maddie? Anyone home?"

"The housekeeper took Maddie to the park."

Rosalind appeared at the railing. She looked quite regal looking down on him. He'd always loved it when she wore jeans as they showed her curves.

"She's been beside herself talking about decorating the tree this evening, so we thought the distraction of friends would do her some good," she said.

"You didn't go with them?" He was surprised, since Maddie had been a human barnacle yesterday.

"I was afraid my sudden appearance might cause others to start gossiping and I didn't want Maddie to feel self-conscious. Besides, I didn't know when you would be home and didn't want to leave you in the lurch."

Like he'd left her by running late and not checking in.

He watched as she made her way down the staircase. "You're annoyed."

"No."

Liar. The frosty coating on her words said as much. He was annoyed with himself, so why shouldn't she be? "I came home as soon as I could," he said. But even to his voice the apology sounded lame.

"Really. I understand," Rosalind said, coming into the living room. She paused at the sofa to pick up his coasts and separate them. "You run a major corporation. It's a very time-consuming position. You can't ignore a problem simply to entertain me."

"Yes, I can." Thomas took the jackets from her and tossed them aside. "And, it's not *'enter-taining.'* I want to spend time with my family."

When they'd first met, he'd told Rosalind that her eyes were the most expressive eyes he'd ever seen. They spoke volumes—sometimes too much—even when she attempted to school her emotions. At the moment he could see a swirl of hurt and disappointment in their brown depths.

God, he was such an idiot. He'd never wanted to see disappointment in her eyes again.

Which meant erasing the feelings as quickly as he possibly could.

An idea struck him. "Get your coat," he told her.

Rosalind blinked. "Excuse me? You just got home and you want to go back out?"

"Together. Yes. I promised shock and awe, remember?"

"There's no need…"

Oh, yes, there was. If he wanted her to stay beyond Christmas anyway. "No protesting. It might be getting a late start but the full charm offensive gets underway right now."

He tried to shoo her toward the closet, but she didn't move beyond crossing her arms in front of her chest. "What about Maddie? She and Mrs Faison will be coming back soon."

"All the more reason for us to move quickly," Thomas replied. There was paper in the Louis XIV desk in the far corner of the room. "I'll leave a note letting Mrs Faison knowing that we're going out for a couple of hours but will be back in plenty of time for tonight's tree-trimming festivities."

"And where exactly are we going?" she asked.

Victory. Her eyes were staring at him with confusion and excitement. He smiled. "Why, to buy a Christmas tree, of course."

Despite the early hour, Covent Garden was awash with both lights and people. Banners of white lights hung in a row along the street, their tiny bulbs waving gently as, beneath them, hordes of shoppers and tourists, arms laden with purchases, paraded past store windows. Feeling like a stranger in a strange land, Rosalind found herself holding Thomas's arm. It wasn't that she found the streets unfamiliar or even frightening. She simply found the crowds overwhelming. So much noise and commotion. Holding on to Thomas's arm kept them from getting separated.

They'd managed to find a suitable tree fairly quickly—a sturdy Douglas fir a few inches taller than Thomas—which was being delivered to their apartment at that very moment. Rosalind had enjoyed watching Thomas and the merchant haggle over the price. The back-and-forth had been more for the sake of show and pride. Still, seeing the fervency with which Thomas tackled negotiations, with his eyes bright and sharp, had made her pity the businesses who met him across the conference table.

"What do you think?" Thomas asked.

"Of what? The decorations? They're lovely."

With their task completed, Rosalind had assumed they would be heading home, but Thomas, still hell-bent on his "full charm offensive," had suggested they walk a bit. *To get you reacquainted with the city*, he'd said.

"I meant, what do you think of London?"

"Ah. It's very crowded."

More than once, Rosalind found herself stepping out of the way of oncoming traffic. "Feels like I'm swimming upstream," she said. "Only in a river of people." The thought recalled other rivers, and she clung closer to him.

"Sorry about that. Product of the season and the time of day. Everyone rushing to get in a little Christmas shopping before they head home."

As if to illustrate her point, a woman in a green wool coat approached, pushing through the crowds. "Sorry," she apologized with a thick foreign accent every time she wedged herself past someone. "So sorry." When the woman reached them, Thomas pulled Rosalind flush to his side. The scent of his coat grounding her.

"Thank you," she murmured.

"You never were a huge fan of crowds. When we finished university, you couldn't wait to get away from people."

Sounded about right. She didn't like crowds. The noise and commotion drained her.

Bringing to mind a question she'd asked the other day. "Is that why we moved north instead of you taking a job with your family's company?"

"It's why *you* moved north," he said. "I moved because I'm not a fan of long-distance relationships. Do you want to head back?"

"Depends. Are we heading somewhere in particular?" From the purposeful way he was cutting through the crowds, he seemed to have a destination in mind.

"You'll see," was his reply. "I don't want to play my entire hand."

Rosalind laughed. You had to give it to him— the man was trying. She had been annoyed earlier. The minute Thomas left for the office, an overwhelming rush of anger and bitterness came over her, same as it had the day before. Why drag her back here if he was going to leave her alone all day?

While a logical part of her argued that corporate emergencies were out of his control, the disappointed part of her was mad he'd gotten her excited about spending time together, then let her down.

Then there was a third part of her that was

ashamed with herself. Maddie was a wonderful child, and she relished every moment with her, but everything they did together felt like it was taking place in someone else's house. When Maddie wanted lunch, it was the housekeeper who made soup and sandwiches. When the phone rang, it was the housekeeper who answered. It was the housekeeper who took Maddie to the park.

She was in stasis, neither a working mum nor a fully hands-on one, and she was bored to death.

Making Thomas's lateness that much more irritating since he was her conduit to any kind of life.

"Hello? Earth to Rosalind?" A gloved hand waved in front of her face. She blinked and realized Thomas was looking down at her, concern in his eyes. How was it that in the middle of a crowded street in the darkness of the winter's twilight he still managed to have the most mesmerizing eyes? This evening the blue was navy again. The color of the ocean. She could see the illuminated banners reflecting in their depths. Like white caps. Wasn't that what she'd thought the first night she'd stared into them?

"Is everything all right?"

"Sorry. I was thinking about Christmas," she lied, her thoughts better left unsaid so as not to ruin the moment. "Trying to imagine what the day will be like. Do you do a big family celebration?"

"Not usually. The Colliers are too spread out to do anything really crazy. There's the company party, which I pushed to January. For obvious reasons." Rosalind's cheeks warmed. "And we'll host a few family members at Christmas dinner. Linus. Susan. My crazy uncle, Seth."

"What about Christmas Eve?"

Strangely, he looked to the sidewalk before speaking. "Well, up until last year we would make toasted cheese sandwiches and drink mulled wine in front of the fireplace. A Christmas campfire, if you will."

"Really?"

Thomas nodded. "It was a tradition we started our very first Christmas and kept going after Maddie was born."

"Sounds fun." She frowned as his full answer struck her. "We didn't have a campfire last year?"

His eyes were still focused on the ground. "Circumstances got in the way."

What circumstances? Rosalind thought of asking, but suspected he'd pivot the conversation the way he did the few other times something awkward came up. She wished she could remember what it was he didn't want her to know.

"My favorite part of the season was always Christmas morning," she told him, doing a little pivoting of her own. "Waking up and finding all the gifts Santa left under the tree. My mother would insist all the gifts were hidden until Christmas morning in order to make what was there look extra spectacular."

Thomas's head jerked up and he stared at her, mouth agape. With a thrill, she realized what she'd just said. After months of blankness, she'd experienced two memories in the same day.

"Looks like coming to London might have been what I needed," she said.

He smiled. A gentle expression that made her insides turn topsy-turvy. "I'm glad."

The two of them rounded a corner, and she saw they were heading to a giant iron-and-glass building housing a marketplace.

Guarding the arched structure, in a giant whisky barrel done up with a red bow, stood a behemoth Christmas tree, at least three times the size of the one destined for their living room. "The tree at Covent Garden," Thomas said. "Thought it might provide inspiration for when we get home. There are other trees around the city, but this one has always been my favorite."

"Why is that?"

The two of them stopped to look skyward. The tree was covered with lights, thousands of them. Red, blue and green, all sparkling in the twilight. Glass balls, nestled in the branches, reflected the colors. It was giant and lovely.

"Not sure," Thomas replied. "I think because of where it is. Whenever I visit the market, I'm reminded that people have been selling their wares on this spot for nearly four hundred years. I know, there's history on every street corner in the city, but this spot…" He pointed to the cobblestone beneath them. "My great-great-whatever-grandfather might have very well stood here selling the first bars of Collier's soap. Bit wild when you think about it."

His words had a bit of awe to them, which

in turn made Rosalind feel the same. "History means a lot to you, doesn't it?"

"You wouldn't say that if you'd seen me fall asleep during sixth form Medieval History," he said with a grin. "But I definitely have an appreciation for the passage of time and continuity."

He led her toward the marketplace entrance. Inside was a sea of stalls filled with crafts and goods of all shapes, sizes and colors. Floral scents mixed with patchouli hung in the air.

Looking to the second floor, its railing strung with lights and garland, she spied a little boy not much older than Maddie. He stood with his chin resting on the rail, eyes focused upward. She followed his gaze and spied row upon row of chandelier lights dripping with mistletoe.

She cast Thomas a sidelong glance.

"Would you look at that," he said with mock innocence. "I had no idea they decked out this entire building with mistletoe. However are you supposed to walk through without someone planting a Christmas kiss on your cheek?"

"However indeed."

The greenery was gorgeous, dangling above them with its lights and red velvet bows. A literal mistletoe canopy for as far as the eye could see.

They strolled down the aisle, stopping every now and then to look at a particularly bright piece of tapestry or sparkling piece of jewelry. Every pause led to an enthusiastic greeting by a stall manager hoping to make a sale. One vendor in particular who sold homemade soap caught Thomas's attention and they spent several minutes discussing the properties of the man's product before Thomas purchased a sample pack. Or more accurately, Thomas spent several minutes discussing the properties of the man's product while Rosalind watched with the same interest as when he'd bought the tree.

The entire time she couldn't stop thinking of the mistletoe hanging overhead. Which only increased her awareness of Thomas's shoulder as they walked side by side. The way the wool of his coat brushed against hers with every step. *Swish. Swish. Swish.*

Suddenly, they stopped. "Wait right here," he said, and he stepped in front of her to block her view. "I'll be right back."

"You're going to leave me in this crowd?"

She looked around at the people jostling within the stalls.

"I'll only be gone for a moment. Don't leave this spot and I'll be right back."

He disappeared before she could protest.

Now what? She couldn't very well stand stock-still like an idiot waiting for Thomas's return. Taking a quick look around, she saw that they'd stopped at a stall selling wooden flowers and crafts. There was a wooden teddy bear puzzle that Maddie would adore. As soon as Thomas returned, she'd take a closer look. Damn if she hated not having any money.

"Oh, my God! It can't be… Rosalind?" A man in a suede jacket and scarf came rushing up to her. Rosalind backed up. When her bottom came into contact with the craft table, she continued leaning backward, trying to increase her distance from the approaching man. She was about to yell for Thomas when she realized the man looked familiar.

He was in one of the photos Thomas had showed her. The one of her colleagues from the university. *Robert? Randall?*

"My God, it is you. How…?"

"Richard." The name popped into her head

and out of her mouth right as the man wrapped his arms around her in a bear hug.

"This is a Christmas miracle. I never thought I'd see you again." His modulated tones settled welcomingly on her shoulders, like a borrowed cardigan on a chilly day. "They told us you were dead."

"They thought I was." Breaking out of his embrace, she filled him in on what'd happened, ending with Thomas finding her at McKringle's. Richard listened intently, then brushed a shock of silver-blond hair from his forehead.

"You mean, you've been in Scotland all this time and none of us knew?"

She nodded.

"And you don't remember anything?"

"Bits and pieces since I've come back to London, but no. I remember you because I saw a photograph…"

With a laugh, he hugged her again. "I'm sorry. I don't mean to be so effusive, but… you're alive! And standing in the middle of Covent Garden!"

"I know." People were starting to look at them. Rosalind let her hair fall down the sides of her face to avoid the stares.

"Thomas must be beside himself. How is he handling the return? Properly contrite and attentive, I imagine."

Contrite was an odd choice of words. "He's doing everything he can to help and being incredibly patient. It isn't easy having a wife who doesn't remember."

"Although he does get to have a clean start," Richard replied.

"What do you—"

"Hello, Sinclair." Thomas's voice had an edge of possessiveness. He walked up from behind and slipped an arm around her waist. Rather than being annoyed Rosalind found herself feeling a bit tingly. "We didn't expect to run into anyone we knew here."

"Rosalind was telling me what happened. I can't believe you didn't let her friends know."

"We sent word to the authorities and the media this afternoon. The rest, I figured, Rosalind could do at her own pace, when she wanted to contact the world. No sense forcing her into situations before she was ready."

"No. I'm sure you wouldn't. Want to force her, that is," Richard replied.

Looking between the two, Rosalind got the

distinct impression their civility was for her ben-
efit. Although why, she hadn't a clue. "Thomas
replaced my phone this morning. I was going to
call people next week once the news got out."

"Meaning I'm the lucky one who got to know
before everyone else. Well, I mean besides your
family," he added, stealing a look at Thomas.

"Speaking of—" Was it her imagination or
did Thomas pull her a little closer? "—we need
to get back home before Maddie tries to climb
the Christmas tree."

"She's antsy enough to do it too," Rosalind
added with a laugh.

Richard gave her one last hug and kiss on the
cheek. "I'll call you tomorrow," he said, "and
we can catch up. This is…well, it's unbelievable, that's what it is. My mind is blown."

Rosalind liked his warm personality. He made
her feel at home even in a strange building. As
Richard walked away, she smiled to herself before stealing a look leftward. Thomas's counte-
nance was the exact opposite. If clenched jaws
could crack, her husband's would be shattered.

"You don't like him," she noted. "How come?"

His jaw muscles relaxed as he let out a long

deliberate breath. "Who, Sinclair? I don't dislike him."

"Then why the face? And don't ask what I mean because it was clear from your expression you weren't happy about something."

"Because…" He angled his body so that, instead of standing side by side, he held her in a semi-embrace. "I'm not ready to share you with the rest of the world."

Whether from his hips close to hers or the mistletoe hanging above them or the gentle whiff of aftershave on his neck, awareness washed over her. She looked up through her lashes. "Then you shouldn't have left me alone in the crowd."

"Ah, but then I couldn't have bought you this." His lifted his free arm to reveal a brown bag. "Merry early Christmas."

It was a geode. Broken open to reveal the pink crystal formations inside. "You told me once you like the pink ones best. That the color's created by—"

"Magnesium." The whispered answer came to her without having to think. "And it's beautiful. Thank you."

"You're most welcome." She looked up to

find his eyes had grown hooded and dark. Her insides started to pulse.

"You know, we are under the mistletoe," he told her.

"I know."

"Be almost sacrilegious if we didn't..."

"Sacrilegious indeed."

His lips brushed against hers. The kiss was soft and sweet, full of the kind of promise that made Rosalind's knees want to buckle.

And then it ended, as a public kiss should. Leaving her tingling and wishing they were alone.

"Let's go home," Thomas said. "We have a tree to decorate."

It wasn't until he led her from the market-place and the taste of his kiss had started to fade that Rosalind realized he hadn't really answered her question about why he disliked Richard.

Unbelievable, thought Thomas, as he studied the crowd ahead of them. Eight-and-a-half-million people in London and they run into Richard Sinclair the first day they leave the apartment.

Then again, maybe it wasn't so unbelievable. Sinclair had been like a bad penny last spring. Why wouldn't he show up when Rosalind returned?

He stole a rightward glance. Rosalind's attention was on the crowd, allowing him a chance to study her profile. He loved the upward sweep of her lashes when her eyes were open wide. He loved their downward sweep when they fluttered closed too, which was what they'd done when he'd kissed her.

Dear God, he'd kissed her. Less than two weeks ago, he would have called the idea a dream. She tasted like… He couldn't come up with a phrase that didn't sound hyperbolic. And the hyperbole? It sounded too pale and inadequate.

Why then wasn't his brain reliving that magical moment instead of ruminating about some chance encounter?

Because Sinclair would be around now, that's why.

Thomas had lied about his feelings toward the man. He definitely disliked Sinclair. Rosalind and other colleagues at the university had been always going on about how funny and smart Sinclair was. Thomas found him irritating. Sinclair struck him as the kind of man who needed to be the smartest and funniest in the room. He lapped up the attention. By last spring, he and Rosalind were thick as thieves. The witty, sympathetic shoulder and the unhappy wife.

All right. Thomas was jealous. Every time Thomas had tried to dig himself out of the hole he'd created, there'd been Sinclair competing for Rosalind's attention.

Richard has tickets to a lecture.

Richard joined us in the park.

We ran into Richard at lunch.

The man had been everywhere and anywhere. He absolutely loved having Rosalind—beautiful, intelligent, daughter-of-geology-royalty Rosalind—as his partner in crime.

Thomas half suspected Sinclair had stoked Rosalind's unhappiness so she would continue to hang around.

"You're staring." Rosalind turned her attention from the crowd to look over at him. "You've grown quiet too. Is everything all right?"

Nothing getting rid of a certain archeologist wouldn't help.

He swallowed the jealous thought. Sinclair was a symptom of their problems, not the cause.

"I'm thinking about what to buy you for Christmas. Going to be hard topping a pink rock." He tossed out the term on purpose. It used to be a joke between them that he couldn't identify specimens by their scientific names.

True to form, Rosalind immediately corrected him. "Manganese carbonate." Then she blushed, realizing the instinctiveness of her answer.

"Whatever. It's still pink. Anyway, I've got the choices narrowed down to either a block of marble, a giant slab of slate or a bucket of pebbles from the pathway in the park. Got a preference?" She turned her head away with an exaggerated sniff. "What?"

"Fine. Don't tell me what you were thinking about. I don't want to know."

"Yes, you do," he teased. "But it's Christmas, which means I get to have a few secrets. Besides—" he leaned in so he could whisper against her ear, loving the way she shivered when his lips brushed against the shell "—anticipation is the best part. So, you'll just have to wait."

"If you say so." She looked up from beneath her lashes. "Guess that means we won't be stopping under any more mistletoe."

Thomas's blood ran straight below his belt. "What?"

"You know, like a penny for your thoughts, only instead…"

The little minx. Putting ideas in his head. He reached for her waist only to have her back away with a giggle.

"Uh-uh-uh," she said, wagging her finger. "You missed your chance. We need to get going home. Someone's waiting to decorate the tree. Besides—" this time she leaned toward him "—didn't you say anticipation is the best part?"

"Looks like one of us is down for the count," Thomas said, pointing to the settee where Maddie lay sprawled on her stomach beneath a blanket. She'd faded while Thomas and Rosalind struggled with the lights. Overloaded with excitement and sugar, she'd crashed hard when the adrenaline wore off.

Rosalind tucked the blanket around her, smiling when the girl mewled and clutched Bigsby closer. "Poor kid. Think she'll be disappointed she missed the finished product?"

"We saved the angel for her," Thomas replied. "Plus, I think she'll be more excited about the possibility of presents under it than stringing lights on the tree." He finished hanging the last ornament, then stepped back. "I have to admit the end result looks quite festive."

Rosalind had to agree. They'd set up the tree in the upstairs library. That was where they always put it. A company-paid decorator did the rest of the apartment, Thomas explained.

The tree, not so tall that Maddie couldn't reach the top from Thomas's shoulders, was set in the corner, hugged by two floor-to-ceiling bookcases. Woolen balls and felt animals—the same ones that had flashed through her mind this morning—hung on the branches.

"It's beautiful," Rosalind said. Simple and homely, unlike the glitzy decorations she suspected would go downstairs. "Explain to me again why we're hiding it up here? Are we afraid of the decorator?"

Her question earned her a chuckle. She'd discovered over the course of the evening that Thomas had a varied and fascinating collection of laughs. There was the amused, from-the-gut laugh he made when playing with Maddie, the slightly mocking laugh he made when he was being sarcastic—that one was reserved for stories about his siblings—and a naughty-sounding laugh that wrapped around her spine whenever they shared a private joke. This particular laugh held a note of question, like he was silently saying, "Maybe."

"The company has hired a decorator to do the president's home for years. Considering we're expected to entertain Collier executives and vendors here, it makes sense.

"Don't worry," he added, sensing how she'd tensed at the idea of playing hostess to a room full of people she didn't remember. "I'd already postponed this year's event until after the New Year due to previous circumstances."

He meant his first Christmas as a widower.

"As for the tree being in the library...it was actually your idea. You wanted a room and a tree more in keeping with your idea of Christmas."

Well, the room definitely fit. The library, while still luxurious, lacked the gilt and glamor of downstairs. The fireplace had a dark mantle, and the overstuffed quarters made the room far more welcoming. She could never picture curling up on the blue velvet sofas downstairs. Yet when taking a seat on the leather love seat, she kicked off her shoes and tucked her legs beneath her without a second thought.

She took a long look at the tree. It too left her with a warm, cozy feeling. The homespun ornaments reminded her of old friends nestled amid the branches.

"Do you think we have enough lights?" she asked.

"Any more and we'll be treading into fire hazard territory," Thomas replied.

He turned off the lights, leaving the room bathed in the glow of hundreds of tiny white points. Rosalind settled back in the corner and sighed. "Gorgeous."

"Couldn't agree more. Though I don't mean the tree." He was leaning in the shadows, drinking her in with a look as warm as the room. "This is the most relaxed I've seen you since we arrived. Being comfortable looks good on you."

"Hard to look uncomfortable when you're surrounded by Christmas."

She turned her face to the fireplace so he wouldn't notice how his flattery affected her. Since their brief kiss at Covent Garden, every word Thomas said left her feeling charged with energy. As though part of her insides had been left dormant and someone—he—had suddenly turned on the switch.

Everything about the evening had been perfect. From the kiss beneath the mistletoe to the crackling fire and carols playing softly on a speaker. The only thing missing was snow falling outside the window.

"Don't the stockings look nice on the mantle?" she asked. Three bright red-and-white knit stockings dangled to the right of the fire.

"I remember how excited you were to hang those stockings our first Christmas." Thomas had moved to the desk where earlier he'd placed a bottle of Chardonnay and a pair of glasses. *Figured we deserved a toast after the tree is finished,* he'd said at the time. Rosalind watched the play of his back muscles as he twisted the corkscrew. When he came home, he'd shed his jacket and tie in favor of another sweater, this one ice blue. The soft wool molded to his frame, accentuating his shoulders. For a lean man, he was surprisingly hard and defined.

Of course, she'd already discovered how defined when he came to her room last night.

"We forgot to buy those holders that slide over the wood, so I ended up hammering a pair of nails into the mantle to hang them up."

It took a moment for her to realize he was still telling the story of the stockings. "Hard to imagine you wielding a hammer." He seemed born to the boardroom.

"Are you joking? I'll have you know I wield the best hammer in the Lake District. Made that table in front of you there."

He had? Looking closer, Rosalind realized the piece was indeed different than the other ones in the room. The sturdy piece was made of darkly stained boards.

"It doubled as a dining room table more than once, especially if you had papers spread all over the actual one. I kept threatening to build you a desk so I could eat my meal without hunching over."

"Why didn't you?"

"Said you didn't want one. You liked working at the table."

"One word from me and you risk becoming Quasimodo? Who knew I had such influence. You didn't mention that in all the information you emailed over."

"Didn't want you getting a big head. Figured you'd find out soon enough." He joined her on the love seat and handed her a glass of wine. "Plus, in case you haven't noticed, you've had your influence somewhat usurped."

"Somewhat, but not completely," she teased. "Means I still have a little power."

"Far more than a little."

As he spoke, he looked at her in a way that made her warm from the inside out. Rosalind sipped her wine and tried not to squirm from the fluttering in her stomach. And who was it that was supposed to have power?

"My papers," she said. "That was my post-graduate work, right?"

"'The cause of graphite deposits in Borrowdale.' Or something like that. I know it was about graphite and Borrowdale."

"Right. Because it's extremely rare to find

graphite deposits hosted in volcanic rock. The only other occurrence is in Spain."

She stopped, her cheeks burning. Thomas was staring at her like he was about to burst out in a grin. "Moments like that have been happening all day," she confessed.

"That's fantastic. At this rate, you'll have your memory back before you know it."

It was hard to tell in the shadows, but he looked genuinely happy about the fact. "I'm not sure I'd pop a cork quite yet. It's only been a handful of snippets. I've yet to remember anything of true importance. Like my parents for example." Or their marriage. Or him, for that matter.

Although the latter seemed to be diminishing in importance as time went on.

"I wish I could help you. I never got to meet your parents. Both of them died before we met."

"The articles you sent about my father made him sound larger than life. My mother too." Experts on photogrammetry and laser scanning, they'd apparently traveled the world lecturing and consulting.

"From the way you always talked, I think they were. I know they were highly regarded and spent a lot of time overseas. You used to say they set a high bar."

"In terms of what? Success?" Rosalind leaned in.

"Probably. Although it wasn't as though they placed high expectations on you. I got the impression the three of you had some wonderful times together."

He turned sideways in his seat and tucked a leg under him in a mirror image of her pose. "I always envied that. Your family connection."

An odd thing to say coming from a man who ran a two-hundred-year-old family business. "You say it as if you and your family aren't close."

"It's complicated," he said, looking down at his wine. "We're more bonded by our family heritage than each other."

"I don't understand."

"The company is the thing that defines and connects us. My father never understood why I moved to Cumbria after graduation instead of stepping into the job waiting for me at the company."

"You said it was because you didn't like long

distance relationships." He hadn't mentioned he'd walked away from his place in the company.

"I don't. I also happened to want to make you happy. The house in Cumbria was the only connection you had left to your parents. So, when you wanted to get out of London and take a job up north, I decided Collier's could find another relative to fill my shoes for a while."

In other words, he'd eschewed his family legacy so she could stay connected to her family's memory. Rosalind's heart caught. "That's quite the romantic gesture."

"Hardly. I loved you and did what I thought would make you happy. I like making you happy, in case you haven't noticed."

And when said like that, it became less grand romantic gesture and more romantic sacrifice. "Were you?" she heard herself ask. "Happy?"

He looked at her from across his glass. "I remember you smiled all the time. I loved seeing you smile like that. Knowing that I was responsible for that smile made feel very proud."

Interestingly, he didn't say *happy*. But they had to have been; they were supposed to move back.

Rosalind watched as he took another drink.

Another set of hands as large as his might make the crystal look fragile, but then another set of hands wouldn't look so elegant.

There was an elegance to how he lifted his neck and swallowed too. As she watched his Adam's apple bob up and down, she shocked herself by imagining tracing her finger along his throat.

And then what? She wasn't sure her heart had caught up to her body.

Thankfully, Thomas, having emptied his glass, was too lost in thought to notice. "Hey," he said, looking at her. "Why don't we tuck Sleeping Beauty into bed? I want to show you something up on the terrace."

It was the view he wanted to show her. Rosalind stepped on to the terrace to see London lit up around her. A personal panoramic postcard. Bundling her coat, she made her way to the railing where Thomas stood waiting. While she'd been putting on her coat, he'd brought up the wine and—somehow—a candle. The items were arranged like a tableau on the ground.

"The city's far less crowded from up here," he said, handing her a glass.

And breathtaking, as well. Across the roof-tops, she could see the Christmas tree by Nelson's Column, as well as the other trees and lights dotting the city. In the distance, Tower Bridge glowed majestically. She could almost see the traffic passing from one end to the other.

"What is it with you and nighttime skies?" she asked. "Seems like you always have me outside in the cold looking at the view."

"Would you rather go back downstairs to the fire?"

"No, not yet." There was something very simple about being outside alone together. With no questions or missing pieces.

"All right, then. How about we drink a toast? To ending the day better than it began."

"Indeed." This morning's disappointment seemed very far away. She tapped the rim of her glass to his, then turned back to the view. "When you told me you were going to charm the socks off me, I didn't believe you, but I have to admit you've been amazingly charming these past few hours."

"Woe on you for doubting."

The sound of laughter drifted upward. Rosalind looked down to see a group walking on the sidewalk across from them. One of them started singing—a raucous, off-tune carol that had the rest of the group joining along. They unknowingly serenaded them until they disappeared around a corner.

As she listened to their song fade in the distance, her skin began to tingle with awareness. Thomas was watching her with an odd gaze.

"I'm sorry about this morning," he said.

"You rallied late in the day. That's what counts."

"I hope so. Thank you. Guess you could say, I'm working extra hard to keep my promises these days."

"A man of his word." The sincerity in his voice touched her in a way that went deeper than attraction. A part of her was unlocking.

"I'm trying to be," Thomas replied. There was more to the answer. Rosalind could sense the unspoken words and sensed they were important. "I want you to know that there's nothing that means as much to me as our being a family again."

"I know."

A beat passed between them and another part

of her unlocked. The world seemed to contract to the two of them and their little terrace.

"Did we really camp out by the fireplace every Christmas Eve?" she asked.

His chuckle was like smoke rising into the darkness. "Those nights are some of my favorite Christmas memories. In fact, I'm pretty sure that's how we got Maddie."

"Oh." Her cheeks burned at the images that came to mind. Wasn't a far jump to go from imagining Thomas stretched out before a fire to imagining…other things.

"Why do you ask?"

"We should do it again this year. Not that," she corrected, earning another sultry chuckle, "but the toasted cheese sandwiches and mulled wine. With Maddie. I don't remember the last time, and I wouldn't mind having the memory again." The fact she was looking at his hands—his strong, capable hands—as she made the suggestion was purely coincidental.

"I wouldn't mind giving you one," he replied with a smile.

Did the man's eyes have to be such a confoundingly beautiful color every time he looked in her direction?

"While we're on the subject..." Without breaking his stare, Thomas set his glass on the railing and stepped closer so that the fog from their breath mingled. "The two of us need to go Christmas shopping for our little angel. Something tells me Santa may want to bring her *slightly more* than cookies."

"Don't forget the friend for Bigsby."

"How could I? We could make an evening of it. Dinner. Dancing. Whatever you'd like."

That his eyes dropped to her lips while he was making his suggestion was definitely not coincidental. Or maybe it was. Rosalind's mouth ran dry regardless. "Are you suggesting a date, Mr Collier?"

"If you're interested, Mrs Collier."

Rosalind ran her tongue across her lips, grateful that he used the moment to bend over and retrieve the wine bottle. How many times had she watched his shoulder muscles flex as he poured liquid? How many times had they bantered? Was it always this natural and easy?

Frustration over her inability to answer clogged her throat. "I wish I could remember when we were dating," she caught herself saying. "I wish I remember a lot of things. Everything, really."

"You will," Thomas assured her. "Look how much has come back just today."

Bits and pieces. And while the flashes were wonderful, they were only glimpses of scenes, not full-blown recollections.

"I know I should be grateful that I'm remembering anything at all. The past months I'd come to terms with the blankness in my head. But now... I want to remember so badly and I can't. I've tried and I can't."

"You always did hate not being in control."

"What?" She started to get angry until she realized he was teasing. His way of keeping her from going down the rabbit hole of frustration. "That is not true," she told him.

"Oh, really? Where do you think our little princess got her tenacious streak?"

"I... That's not the same thing."

Thomas arched a brow.

"It's not," she persisted.

"How hard have you been trying to remember since yesterday?"

Rosalind thought of all the photographs she'd stared at over the last twenty-four hours. Hoping for some glimmer of recognition. "Not that hard."

He chuckled again, the throaty sound pooling in her stomach in spite of her albeit-slight annoyance. "It's all right," he told her. "I happen to like that tenacity. It's why you're sitting here with me tonight. It takes true strength to survive what you've been through. But then you've always been a strong woman. Determined."

His fingers caught in her hair, combing through the strands. "I should have realized rushing water and a damaged car couldn't stop you."

This time she chuckled. Low and shy. "You make me sound like way more than I am."

"Not to me," he whispered.

Rosalind's heart fluttered. He was looking at her with such sincerity and wonder. Like in her dream, she felt pulled under. Drowning in a flood of nerves and awareness. She reached for her wine.

Why? What was she afraid of? They were married. Shouldn't she feel this kind of intense attraction?

Perhaps the answer wasn't to avoid, but to explore?

Thomas's lips glistened from the wine. She brushed at the sheen with her fingers. "Kiss me," she whispered.

CHAPTER SEVEN

HAD HE HEARD RIGHT?

For the past two hours Thomas had been fighting the urge to touch his wife. Every accidental brush of their fingers, every shy sideways glance had him aching with the desire to wrap his arms around her. The need wasn't even sexual. He simply wanted to feel her closeness. The way it had been before everything fell to pieces.

Her request sounded too good to be true.

There was desire in her darkened eyes though. And the fingers tracing a feathery path along his jaw had him stifling a groan.

Who was he to pass up the moment?

Shifting closer, he trailed the back of his hand down her cheek before sliding his fingers into her hair. He'd always loved how easily the strands slipped through them.

"I thought you'd never ask," he whispered.

She sighed, and he touched his lips to hers. Gently. Once. Twice.

On the third kiss, her lips parted and their mouths slanted together as though they'd never been apart. They moved in perfect rhythm.

Rosie, Rosie, Rosie. His brain chanted her name like a mantra. How he'd missed her. She might not remember him, but her body knew. She surged into him, her hands tangling in his hair.

"It's been so long," he whispered. "I missed you so much." He backed her against the rail, pressing into her so she could feel how badly he needed her. In return, she moaned and clutched his shoulders. The soft sound was nearly his undoing. If they didn't head downstairs, he was going to lose it right there on the terrace.

Peppering her face with butterfly kisses, he scooped her into his arms.

"Thomas, wait."

He looked down at her glazed expression. Her eyes were hooded, dark with desire, but something was off. The trembling in her body wasn't from desire.

Slowly he lowered her to her feet. Even in the

dark, he knew there was apology in her eyes. "I'm sorry," she whispered.

She needn't be. It was too soon. She'd wanted a kiss, and in obliging, he had forgotten himself. He stroked the hair from her cheek, letting his thumb graze her swollen lips. "You'd better get inside before you get cold."

Rosalind closed the door to her bedroom and shut her eyes. What had she been thinking? Asking Thomas to kiss her. The man had real feelings and memories. Until she was certain she could return them, what right did she have to experiment with their attraction?

Then again, she hadn't expected the attraction to flare so dramatically. When he'd kissed her, it was as if she'd been ripped open emotionally. Everything—his touch, his taste—had overwhelmed her. Flooded her with sensations she couldn't explain. Without context they terrified her.

There were still too many questions. Instinct nagged at her that there was something being left from the picture Thomas painted. Then there was her run-in with Richard. While 99 percent of her had been consumed by Thomas's kisses, there was a tiny voice whispering, *Contrite, contrite*, in her ear. What had Richard been talking about?

She needed more. Time. Information. Memories. Her brain needed to catch up with her body.

In the meantime, she'd try to forget how Thomas's kiss seemed to reach to her soul. Not to mention the pain she saw in his face when she'd walked away.

Another emergency. Naturally. Thomas threw his phone on to the bed where it bounced off a pillow and became lost in the covers. He was already in a horrible mood thanks to a rotten night's sleep. He did not need another problem dragging him into the office on yet another day he should be spending with his wife. He wanted—no, he needed to see where they stood after last night's kiss. He needed to know if his fears regarding her retreat were real or not.

The question had kept him up half the night. He'd tried to talk to her last night, but when he'd knocked on her door, she hadn't answered.

Did she regret asking him to kiss her? That's what he feared. At the time, he'd hoped the passion might jostle her memory, remind her how good they'd been. But last night, standing on the wrong side of her bedroom door, a different fear had gripped him. What if her feelings were truly gone? Not lost in amnesia but gone. What if she'd given up on them before that weekend she'd spent in Cumbria, and no amount of recollection could bring the feelings back?

Those were the questions he'd hoped to explore this morning until the blasted phone rang. Honest to God, what would this company do without him?

What would he do without Collier's?

Survive, same way he did before. He answered his own question. He didn't *need* Collier's. He needed Rosalind. And he intended to show her how much.

But first, he had to put out today's office fire.

By the time he was out of the shower and dressed, Rosalind's bedroom door was open. He found her in the library with Maddie. The two of them were in bathrobes and were giggling as Rosalind had the little girl hoisted on her shoulders. Although their backs were to him, he could see the angel tree-topper in Maddie's hand. She was stretching to reach the top branch to no avail. The tree had, after all, been bought with his shoulders in mind, not Rosalind's.

"It's no use," he heard Rosalind say. "I'm too short. We'll have to wait until your father's done talking on the phone."

Thomas's conscience pricked and he vowed to get his business done as quickly as possible.

"Looks like someone needs to grow a couple of inches," he said.

"Daddy. We're doing the angel."

"So I see." Catching Maddie by the waist, he lifted her up and over Rosalind's head and on to his shoulders. Stepping as close as possible, he waited patiently for her to arrange the angel.

"Thank you," Rosalind said once they were finished. Maddie immediately ran off to retrieve Bigsby, leaving them alone. "She woke up determined to finish what she didn't get to accomplish last night."

"Funny, so did I."

While she smiled at the remark, Rosalind backed away before he could kiss her good-morning. "Sorry. Last night was—"

Please don't say a mistake.

"—a mistake. I got caught up in the wine and

the moment and pushed for something before I was ready."

"It was a kiss," Thomas said. In the sense that Collier's soap was just another soap. But for her sake, he tried to downplay it.

"It's just too soon," she repeated. "Everything is new, except it's not new and I can't tell if a feeling is from memory or if it's happening now. Or maybe it's not a feeling at all—I'm just forcing the emotion."

She turned to him her eyes shining. "Am I making sense?"

Yes, she was. Unfortunately. Hurt like a kick between the legs, but he understood. "I shouldn't have pushed you last night."

She gave him a sideways look. "Appreciate the chivalry, but I was the one who asked you."

"For a kiss. Not an explosion of pent-up need." Seeing her breath quicken and the red seep down her neck and into her cheeks, Thomas knew he'd succeeded in painting an accurate picture.

"Apology accepted," she murmured.

"I promised you before that I wouldn't make you be anything you weren't ready to be. That includes doing anything before you're ready as well. Of course, I might take a few hundred cold showers."

"Only a few hundred?" she asked with a laugh. "I'm insulted."

"Did I say 'hundred?' I meant a few hundred thousand."

"Better." Their eyes connected and they smirked broadly at one another. "Seriously, though," Rosalind said. "You don't mind going slow?"

Unable to help himself, he caught her chin and, even though it probably violated her request, thumbed her plump lower lip. "I'll let a snail beat me, if that's what you need."

"Thank you." To his surprise, she rose on tiptoes to press a kiss to his cheek.

"You look dapper this morning," she said afterward. Since he hoped not to be long, he'd forgone his suit in favor of a jacket and sweater.

Rosalind's hands smoothed his lapel while he focused on trying to not touch where she'd kissed him, like a teenage boy.

"I feel underdressed—oh."

It was like a switch being turned off. One moment her eyes were sparkling, the next they'd grown distant and hurt. How many times did that look anger him last spring? And haunt him over the summer?

"I'll be as fast as I can," he said. Inside, he kicked himself knowing how many times he'd said the same line in the past and failed to follow through. As many times as he'd said the next line: "I wouldn't go in if this wasn't important."

In his mind, he heard her familiar reply. *It's always important.*

This Rosalind, the one who didn't remember her lines, shrugged. Then she said coolly, "No need to rush on our account. Maddie and I will find something to do."

Thomas was wrong. She did remember her lines. "This really is important. There's another snag with the new product line." He needed production to recalculate its estimates and personally reassure his European distributors. "Collier's future depends on my making sure this new product is a success."

"I know. It's fine."

No, it wasn't fine. He wanted to be here with them. Did Rosalind realize he wasn't abandoning them by choice? That he had to be the one making the decisions? He was so close to getting Colliers on stable ground. Then things would be different. *He* would be different. If only she could see that he truly had learned his lesson when she walked out last spring.

But then, how could she see anything when it looked like he was repeating the same mistakes? And how could he tell her when doing so would only lead to the one conversation he wanted to avoid?

So he said nothing, choosing to stand in the middle of the room while she needlessly fluffed a cushion from the sofa.

"Why don't I work here?" The compromise smacked him on the side of the head. "I can do my business over the phone as easily as I can in person." For crying out loud, half the business was by phone. It was so obvious he didn't know why he didn't think about it before.

"I'll wrap up as quickly as possible, and then we can spend time together. Maybe take you round to your office and other favorite haunts— Dammit." He'd forgotten.

Rosalind turned around.

"I have to sign off on some documentation. I'll have Andrew bring over the final copy once we're finished." He reached for his phone.

"Don't," Rosalind said. "Don't inconvenience some employee so you can barricade yourself in the library all day."

"It won't be more than an hour or two. Three, tops."

"If that's what you want," Rosalind replied. She turned back to the cushions.

This was not the morning Thomas wanted, with tension hanging thick in the air. They might as well be back to last spring. If only he could close the curtains and bring back last night.

"I'll text and let you know what time I'll be home." Crossing the divide, he leaned in and kissed her cheek. A tiny sigh escaped her lips. "I won't be long," he said, his forehead resting against her temple. "I promise."

With that, he went to find his daughter and tell her the same.

Rosalind waited until she heard Thomas leave the room, then punched the cushion. She was being childish. She was disappointed that he was going into work instead of spending time with her, and acting irrationally. The man ran a company. Corporate emergencies happened. It just felt like emergencies happened a lot since she came home.

Didn't excuse her from acting their daughter's age. What did she expect? First she tells the man she didn't remember him, then that she wanted the right to leave after the New Year. To top it all off, she kissed him, then told him she needed to take it slow. And now she was annoyed he wasn't ignoring his business to be with her.

Like she said, irrational.

What disturbed her most, however, was the intensity of her irritation. Her hurt felt old and festering. What's more, the bad mood was causing a headache to form at the base of her neck. Great. A migraine. Was she prone to them, or were they to be another gift from her accident? She pinched the bridge of her nose.

For crying out loud, Rosalind, what do you expect me to do? We're talking about my family's company!

I thought we *were your family.*

The rest of the argument faded away, leaving anger behind. She was right. Her anger was old. Was she overreacting because of an event in the past?

Pinching harder, she tried to bring the memory back. Nothing. Much as she hated her inability, she couldn't force something before its time.

Deciding she needed a cup of coffee, she left the library and headed downstairs. The change in atmosphere astounded her. From comfortable to cold in forty steps. Her neck and shoulders tensed. The room made her feel like she was wearing the wrong skin.

The dining room table was already set with coffee and her pastries. Someone would come out shortly to see if she needed anything else. There was "someone" to do everything. She'd felt like an interloper baking in the kitchen yesterday.

It wasn't the décor that felt ill fitting. It was the whole lifestyle.

All of a sudden she felt very alone, stuck in a large house with no one to explain her feelings to. *I want to go home*, she thought. Only she was home. That was the problem.

The phone Thomas had given her was in the pocket of her robe. She'd been about to call Chris and Jessica to give them an update when

Maddie had asked about the angel. She needed to hear the sound of their voices more than ever.

Voice mail. They must have gone early to the fish market. Chris never missed it. She left a quick message telling them she'd call back later. Hopefully, her voice sounded upbeat enough. She didn't want to worry him.

The phone was barely back in her pocket before it rang.

"I said I'd call back," she laughed. "You didn't have to drop everything."

"Oh, good. You're awake. I wasn't sure if it was too early to reach you."

Rosalind looked at the caller ID, and then smiled. Richard. Nice to know there was someone eager for her company. "Good morning to you too. I'm glad you called."

"The announcement about your return was on the news last night although the story didn't give much detail. Just that you were found in Scotland and the family was only recently notified about your survival. Apparently, Thomas asked for privacy, but I assume that didn't mean friends. Well, maybe he did, but I don't care. I've missed you way too much."

Another person declaring feelings she couldn't

recall. "I'm really sorry. There are so many things I don't remember."

"There's no need to apologize. You have amnesia. Ask me anything you want, and I'll try to fill you in best I can. That is, if you'd like me to."

Oh, would she ever. "Thank you."

For the next half hour, Richard told Rosalind about her job at the university, her research and its demise. "We were all furious when you lost your funding. Losing you was like a giant hole had been carved into the offices. Texting you was not nearly the same as stealing you away for three-martini lunches."

"We had three-martini lunches?"

"Not really. More like one beer and chips at the pub, but they were glorious lunches regardless. Although I'm not sure your husband was too fond of them."

Instinct suggested Richard was right. Clearly, there wasn't any love lost between the men. This was her chance to find out why. "About Thomas," she said. "Why did you say he must be contrite now that I'd returned? What exactly would he need to feel apologetic about?"

On the other end, there was silence as he chose his words. "Well…" he began.

Rosalind listened intently.

"I figured out the Collier curse," Linus announced as he entered the conference room.

"Our lack of doors with locks?" Thomas replied.

"Very funny."

"I'm not joking. I don't have time for your witty insights right now. I have a video conference with our French partner in ten minutes." Then he had to get home with at least part of the day to spare. How was it lawyers could turn one small problem into a multi-day disaster?

Linus being Linus, he didn't care what Thomas had on his plate. He pushed Thomas's electronic tablet toward the center of the conference table and perched himself on the edge. "Genetics," he said.

"I was in the middle of reviewing figures," Thomas replied.

"I'm serious, Thommy-boy. It dawned on me this morning. The Colliers lack the moderation gene."

"You're going to be lacking something else if you don't move. I need to have those figures."

Never mind. He'd walk around to the other side and grab the blasted tablet himself.

"Did you know that I haven't had a day off in over two years?" Linus asked.

"So, take a few days off. No one's stopping you."

"You're making my point. I'm stopping me. I keep telling myself that taking time off is only worthwhile if I take a true break. I'm talking a month or more. And how can I take that much time if the company's in flux?"

"The cost of sharing a name with the company," Thomas replied. "Why do you think I'm here instead of with my wife?" When yours were the shoulders people relied on to carry the burden, there were some luxuries you couldn't afford.

The thought left an uneasy feeling in the pit of his stomach.

"Then how come other executives manage? They manage to have lives. Vacations. Families. And yet, you, me, Susan—we don't. Ergo, the Colliers must be genetically incapable of work-life moderation. That is our curse."

"No," Thomas replied. "My curse is having a brother interrupting my business and preventing me from getting home so I can have work-life balance." This morning's conversation with Rosalind haunted him, and Linus's comments weren't helping.

"As soon as I finish this call, I'm going home. And, for your information, I plan to *stay* home. I'm going to turn off my phone, unplug my email and go dark until after Christmas."

Linus snorted.

"You don't believe me."

"Oh, I believe you."

"Then what's the problem?"

"You proved my point. All in or all out. Genetics, bro. The three of us need to figure out a way around them."

Thomas's fingers curled around the tablet. This morning's conversation with Rosalind haunted him. He was standing at a very important crossroad where he could either repeat his mistakes or work to bring her closer. Now was not the time for one of Linus's theories. Especially one that cut so close.

He needed to go home and spend time with

his wife before the distance he sensed this morning grew stronger.

Ninety minutes later, Thomas entered his apartment with renewed resolve. He'd finished his video conference in record time, but he'd made it clear to the entire staff that barring a national emergency he was not to be disturbed. From here on, his focus would be on Rosalind and only Rosalind.

"I'm home!" he called, closing the door. Quiet answered him. "Rosalind?"

Maddie's coat was gone from the closet, as was Mrs Faison's. They must have gone to the park again.

He headed upstairs to find Rosalind's bedroom door shut. Memories of other days with closed bedroom doors caused the hair on the back of his neck to start to rise. Twisting the knob, he opened the door and slowly stepped inside.

"Is everything all right?"

The shades had been pulled, filling the room with shadows. Rosalind lay on top of the covers, a hand covering her eyes. For a moment, Thomas simply stood, taking in how beautiful she looked in the dim light. Once upon a time, he'd have slipped into the space next to her and smoothed the hair from her scalp. Hell, even yesterday he might have considered the gesture. After this morning, however, he found himself rocking uncertainly on his feet.

"Rosie?" he whispered, afraid to speak loudly and spoil the scene.

"I'm awake," came the monotone reply.

He allowed himself to move closer until he settled on the edge of the bed. Although his hands wanted to reach out, he clasped them between his knees. "Migraine?" he asked.

"How observant of you."

"Is there anything I can do?"

"Sure." She opened her eyes. In spite of the dimness, Thomas could feel their chill. A side effect of the migraine. Had to be.

"What do you need? Water? A blanket."

"I was thinking more about answers."

Answers? About what?

"After you left, I had another flash of memory," she told him.

"You did?"

"We were having an argument."

"Oh." He tried to keep his features schooled

in a semblance of calm despite the uneasiness creeping down his back. "That shouldn't be a surprise. Married people argue all the time."

"I think this was more than a marital spat. We were arguing about work. About your work and your complete disregard for your family."

There it was, the first brick being pulled from what little foundation he'd managed to build. This was exactly the conversation he'd feared. "I'm not sure what to say." That she was viewing the situation through a small filtered lens? That she was misreading circumstances?

This was what he got for gambling on his charm as a distraction.

Blasted hindsight was always twenty-twenty, wasn't it? Standing, he walked across the room to where the dark brown drapes shrouded the window. He should open them so they could have a proper talk in the light of day, but somehow it seemed more fitting to continue in the dark.

She was waiting for him to respond.

"We did argue about my job," he said. "I told you that when we first moved to London, we planned on the move being temporary. Neither of us were prepared for my father to take a bad turn. Or for how many hours I would have to put in taking over. There was a little…friction."

"More than a little friction," she corrected.

"We—"

"I talked to Richard Sinclair."

Thomas should have known. "And I'm sure he was more than eager to fill in your memory, wasn't he?"

"Why wouldn't he? He's my friend."

A friend who preferred that his playmate didn't like spending time with her husband.

There was a crack in the curtains. He pried the cloth apart and looked down on St. James's Street. Behind him, the mattress squeaked as Rosalind shifted her weight. "Richard told me that before the accident we'd been having problems."

"We were going through a rough patch."

"He said we'd been having problems for quite some time. That after you took over your father's company, you became a completely different person, forgetting everything that was important to you. To us."

"This wasn't about us. I was trying to ensure the survival of the company. For Maddie."

"I'm sure our five-year-old daughter will be

thrilled to know she has money in the bank the next time you're unavailable."

"Don't." Thomas whirled around. "Don't you dare suggest I've been unavailable. I have been available every day for the last six months. I didn't see your friend Richard running over here to help out in your memory."

Rosalind was sitting up against the headboard. She had her arms folded across her chest. "Have you looked at the pictures on the mantle recently?"

The abrupt change of topic threw him, as did her sudden change of tone. She was using the same composed, purposeful tone he used when about to prove a point.

"Not recently. Why?"

"There's one on the far left. A formal shot of the three of us. Maddie's wearing a pastel dress."

"Last year's Easter portrait," he replied, knowing the photo immediately. He kept it out year-round because it was the last shot taken of the three of them together. "What about it?"

"I was studying it this afternoon. Comparing it to the others. You and I look miserable."

"We're smiling."

"We're smiling at the camera." Rosalind looked askance at him. "Our mouths have smiles but we aren't smiling."

Thomas didn't argue. Why bother? He knew exactly what she meant, and she was right.

"I had the same expression in the other recent photos you showed me. From your phone."

The fund-raiser. He remembered it well. Rosalind had been surprised he'd attended, had almost seemed to resent that he had.

"So, I need to ask." She turned so they could look each other in the eye. "How bad were our problems?"

Did he deflect the question? Turn the conversation to a different topic and buy himself a little more time?

After all, avoidance worked so well the last time.

No, he couldn't. They'd exchanged vows. He'd promised to love and honor. Whatever the fallout, he owed her an honest answer.

It was time to face the music.

"Bad," he answered. "Things were very bad."

CHAPTER EIGHT

"I KNEW THERE was something you weren't telling me."

Even suspecting the answer, hearing Thomas say it out loud crushed her. During their call, Richard had reluctantly filled her in on the fact her marriage had been rocky. Thomas was a workaholic, he'd said, who continually placed business over family. He'd eagerly fallen back into his wealthy and privileged lifestyle, completely ignoring Rosalind's wishes for a simple, uncomplicated life.

"Whenever I mentioned Cumbria, I could feel this shadow," she said. "Foolish me, I thought I was bringing up bad memories, but really you didn't want to talk about the place because you were afraid I'd remember wanting a divorce."

Thomas paled.

"Richard told me," she said.

"Of course he did. Good friend that he is."

"At least he told me the truth, unlike my husband."

She was furious. Too furious to rant and rave. How dare he bring her back here and make her think they were some happy little family? Seduce her into kissing him with his soulful blue eyes?

"All that information. Not one mention that we were separated."

"Because we weren't," Thomas shot back. "We weren't separated.

"You said you needed a couple of days alone to think. Without Maddie or me around to distract you. So you went to Cumbria for the weekend. A weekend, no more. You didn't want to leave Maddie for longer. And then you had your accident. But despite what Richard thinks, we—you—never made any decisions."

She looked down at the ring on her left hand. "I took off my wedding ring."

"Which you always did when working in the field. That part is the truth. I'd… I told myself you took off your ring before you drove to Scotland because you thought you might be outside."

Or had she decided they were over? Had she

driven north looking for a new home for her and Maddie? Rosalind twisted at the band. The pillow beside her smelled like Thomas. Funny how that was the first detail to pop into her head, but then she had spent the night with her face buried in the scent.

"Two weeks." Her voice sounded flat to her ears. "We've been talking for two weeks. Why didn't you say something?"

"What was I supposed to say? I'd been mourning you for months. Suddenly, I find you in Scotland and I was overjoyed. All I could think about was the fact you were alive."

A tiny bit of her anger leaked away at his answer. Just a tiny bit however, because once the shock had worn off, he still had had plenty of opportunities to fill in the pieces.

What hurt the most was that her heart had started to open to him. There had been so much promise in his kiss, in his eyes.

"Were you ever going to tell me?" she asked. "Or were you just going to wait until the memory popped back into my head?"

Across the room, Thomas studied the carpeting.

"Great. In other words, you were going to

play me for a fool." Again, she thought of their kiss, and her heart cracked a little. Worse, he didn't have a single word of defense.

She lay back down, turning her back to the windows. "I think you should leave."

"I thought if you stayed long enough and we spent time together, you would see things differently. That you'd see that I was different."

His confession wasn't what Rosalind expected.

"Different how?" she asked, rolling over.

"When you went missing, I thought the guilt would cut me off at the knees. It was my fault you went away. I'd made the same mistake my father and grandfather had made, and as a result Maddie didn't have a mother. It made me realize that I should have paid more attention to what mattered.

"When you returned and you didn't remember, I realized I had a second chance. I wasn't trying to lie to you, Rosie. I swear."

No, lying wasn't his style. She didn't need her memory back to know he wasn't malicious. Avoidance of the issue made much more sense. "I believe you."

His face brightened. "You do?"

"Yes."

"You have no idea—"

"But." She stopped him before he could come closer. "It doesn't change anything. That things are different."

"But you just said you believed me."

"Your apology," she said. "But are circumstances truly different?"

"Of course they are."

"Really? What do you call today? Or yesterday? Or the day before that? For crying out loud, Thomas, you couldn't stay away from the office when your wife returned from the dead."

From the way he looked away, she could tell her point had met its mark. "I admit, the past couple of days there have been some emergencies, but I promise there won't be anymore."

"Until there is one," she replied.

"You don't understand…"

A chip of conversation popped into her head. *You don't understand. Collier's needs me right now.* It set her teeth on edge. Her anger returned. He'd dragged her from the home and life she loved, only to abandon them for an executive office.

As far as she could tell, he still was.

"Actually, what I understand is why I needed a weekend away," she told him.

Another direct hit. This time he winced. And, foolish her, she wanted to literally drop everything, to rush and console him.

How could she feel sympathy for him when she was the victim?

"You want to separate. Is that what you're saying?"

Was it? "I need space," she said, déjà vu overwhelming her. "Time to think and learn about my life again. Remember my life again. Or have you forgotten that little problem?"

"I haven't forgotten."

Silently they assessed one another, the clock on her nightstand ticking off the passing seconds. In what was an incredible display of emotional management, Thomas eased the tense set of his shoulders, switching from apologetic husband to a man in control. A company president. "Nor have I forgotten you promised to stay until after the New Year," he said finally.

So that was his issue. Rosalind keeping her promise. Ironic.

"Don't worry. I have no intention of ruining Maddie's Christmas. I'll stay here until January. After that, I think it might be a good idea if she and I stayed somewhere else for a while. To give us time to bond and for me to…think."

"Fine," Thomas replied.

"Fine," Rosalind repeated. She was trying not to let the gleam in his eye make her insides squirrelly. "Now, if you'll excuse me, I need to lie down. My head is killing me."

She rolled back over, keeping her eyes closed until she heard the bedroom door shut. Only then did she give a soft sob.

One conversation and they were back to where they were six months ago. Thomas couldn't say he didn't have it coming. He should have been honest about the state of their marriage when he'd found her in Scotland.

Face it. You were too afraid she'd slip out of your life again.

"Aargh!" He scrubbed his hands over his face. How did he let the best thing that ever happened to him get so messed up?

He headed into the living room and found himself wandering toward the fireplace. Next week, the decorator would be in to overdeck the halls. Thomas knew because his assistant had marked the date in his calendar. If it was like last year, that meant lots of draped greenery and candles. In the meantime, the photo Rosalind had been talking about, the Easter portrait, remained where Rosalind said it was. The three of them were seated in the living room, Maddie perched between her parents. It had taken forever to keep her from squirming. Rosalind looked as beautiful as always with her hair swept back and her soft pink dress. Thomas wondered if he would ever look at her and not think she was the most beautiful woman in the world.

Once his heart finished skipping a beat, he took a closer look. And frowned. Rosalind was right: they looked miserable.

"No more," Thomas said to himself as he flipped the photo facedown. He wasn't done fighting. Not by a long shot. It might mean changing his timetable as far as Collier's was concerned, but dammit he would do whatever it took to keep his marriage alive. If that meant risking Collier's legacy, so be it.

CHAPTER NINE

"Mummy, Mummy, Mummy…" Maddie's whisper was more of an excited squeal. Bouncing up and down, she yanked on Rosalind's sweater. "He's here!"

"What?" Rosalind turned her attention from the email Richard just sent her. "Who's here?"

"Santa! He's downstairs. Do you think he's here to check on me? I said he didn't have to bring me anything because you came home."

"Slow down and catch your breath before you turn blue. What's this about Santa Claus?" She swore the little girl was getting more wound up by the day. The abundance of Christmas cookies and the arrival of a fifteen-foot-tall tree in the living room didn't help. At this point, the girl would pop a spring by Christmas Eve.

"He's downstairs," Maddie insisted. "I saw him talking to Daddy."

She sighed. Probably someone Thomas hired to spread Christmas cheer. Since their argument the other day, she swore he was proving some kind of point by being home every day. Of course, being Thomas, he couldn't simply be in the apartment. He had to fill the apartment with his presence. His laugh would insist on drifting down the corridor. The air pulsated with his proximity. The other day she swore she could smell his scent on every piece of furniture, including her bedsheets.

And if that wasn't bad enough, she'd had to spend last night by the fireplace listening to him reading Christmas stories to Maddie. He was marvelous with her. It was obvious the two of them had developed a special bond during her absence. Watching him with her last night, his voice gentle and sweet, her heart had skipped more than a few beats. And now, he'd arranged for Santa.

This was all well and good, but as Richard's conversation reminded her, once he'd proved his point and won her over, Thomas would revert right back to form. *Don't you deserve someone who understands what you need?* he'd asked.

All right, that particular line was a bit presumptuous.

"Mummy. Come on. Before he leaves." Maddie grabbed her hand and started pulling her toward the library door. "I think he's here on a special mission because he's not in his suit, but I recognized him anyway."

"Slow down. What do you mean he's not in his—Chris!" She called the man's name from over the banister.

He and Thomas stood with their backs to the stairway admiring the Christmas tree. Even so, she'd recognize him anywhere. At the sound of his name, he turned around, his bearded cheeks splitting into a giant smile. "Merry Christmas, Lammie!" He stretched out his arms. Rosalind hurried down the stairs and into the waiting hug. He smelled of peppermint and Scotch pine.

"It's so good to see you," she murmured against his chest.

"It's good to see you too. I was just telling your husband that I had business in the city, so I thought I'd come by and see what my favorite waitress was up to."

She drew back in his arms. "Why didn't you say something when we talked the other night?"

"I wanted it to be a surprise."

"Well, you succeeded." As she hugged him a second time, she glanced past him to Thomas who was watching them with a wistful expression.

"Mummy, you know him?" Maddie was looking up at Chris with giant eyes.

"She thinks you're Santa Claus," Rosalind whispered.

"Is that so?" Immediately Chris knelt down, his eyes twinkling merrily. "How are you today, Miss Madeline?"

Upon hearing him say her name, Maddie's eyes grew even larger, if such a thing was possible. Rosalind had to stifle a giggle.

"First time I've seen her speechless," Thomas remarked.

"Your mum and dad tell me you've been a very good girl this year. Is that true?"

Maddie nodded. "No matter what Jaime Kensington says," she added.

"I'm glad to hear it," Chris said with a chuckle. "I came by to see your mummy and make sure she's being good, as well. Is she?"

"Uh-huh. Daddy too. Last night he read me a story about a mouse who saved Christmas, and we had Christmas cookies."

So much for speechless.

"Cookies, you say." He gave a chuckle. "I don't suppose you have any more, do you? I've always had a fondness for Christmas cookies."

"We have tons. I'll get you a whole plate."

"I'll go with her," Thomas volunteered. "I asked the housekeeper to make tea."

"A lovely girl, Lammie," Chris said once they were out of earshot. "Sounds like she's got a bit of a brain in her head too."

"More than a bit," she said. "There are times when I can't believe I could have forgotten…" Damn. She thought she'd pushed past the guilt, but a lump found its way to her throat anyway. "Sorry."

"No need. You've been through a lot. Emotions are bound to creep up on you now and again."

"You can say that again," she replied with a sniff. "Sometimes I don't know what I'm feeling."

"What do you mean?"

"Nothing. I'm babbling is all." The last thing she wanted was to spoil his visit by causing him to worry.

"Now, don't go telling me it's nothing." Chris

arched a bushy brow. "I'm Santa, remember? I can tell when someone's not telling me the whole story."

"I thought your powers were limited to judging naughty and nice."

"I have all sorts of powers," he told her. "Why don't you sit down and tell me how you're really doing?"

As briefly as she could, since the others were due back, she told him about the separation. "Turns out we weren't the happy family Thomas claimed we were."

"He certainly seemed happy to see you in the restaurant," Chris said. "Overjoyed."

"Sure, because he'd thought I was dead. But that doesn't erase the problems we were apparently having. According to Richard—"

"Who?"

"A colleague of mine from the university. He's been helping me fill in some of the blanks. What's wrong?"

He was frowning. "Nothing's wrong," he said. "Far be it from me to tell you how to handle your situation, but I have to say I'm surprised you're not asking Thomas to fill in these blanks."

"Thomas has filled in some, as well," she replied, a little more defensively than she would have liked. She didn't want to tell him that with Thomas, every trip down memory lane left her topsy-turvy with emotions.

The sound of footsteps and chatter stopped them from saying any more. A second later, Maddie skipped into the room, a piece of paper clutched in one hand and a cookie in the other. Thomas trailed behind her carrying the tea set.

"We picked out three kinds of cookies," Maddie announced. "The ones with the jam are my favorite."

"They look delicious," Chris replied. "Jessica sent some of her famous shortbread for me to give you, but..." He patted his belly. "It was a long flight."

"We'll tell her they were delicious regardless, won't we, Rosie? Although I think she'll learn your secret when your trousers are suddenly too tight." Thomas winked in her direction as he reached for a biscuit. Rosalind cursed her stomach for fluttering.

"I'm afraid Jessica's been onto my secret for years," Chris said. "I gain weight every December."

No wonder, Rosalind thought as she eyed the stack on his plate. She poured the adults their tea and added a small amount of milk to a teacup for Maddie.

As she was handing Chris his cup—in between cookies—he remarked, "The whole town is buzzing about the soap factory's expansion. Your investment is going to do quite a lot for the community."

Thomas was investing in McDermott's soap factory?

"That was the emergency meeting we had the other day," Thomas replied. "Although to be fair, the bank is putting up the funds for the expansion. Collier's simply subcontracted them to do business with us. I've got to admit I was very impressed with their capabilities. With luck, this expansion will be a good decision for both of us."

"I know Ryan McDermott's eager to prove your confidence right."

"I'm eager for him to prove it, as well. I'd hate to be the Collier who killed the company." He laughed as he made the comment, but Rosalind noticed his smile wavered at the edges.

"Two centuries is a long time for a company

to survive, that's for sure." Chris clicked his tongue. "Here I thought my one little restaurant was a handful. I can't imagine keeping a company afloat for that long. Soap must run in your veins."

This time, Thomas's laugh was fuller and less tremulous. "Wouldn't surprise me. I wasn't much older than Maddie when I made my first scented soap."

"Really?" Rosalind was surprised.

Chris took another cookie from his stack. "Pretty young age to be working in a laboratory."

"Oh, no, we weren't in the lab, although my brother Linus probably would have loved if we were. This was the company museum."

"Collier's has a museum?" Rosalind wondered what else about the company she didn't remember.

"A small one. On the first floor of the corporate building. It's mostly articles and newsreels about Collier's contribution through history. Our role in the war efforts and things like that. But there are a couple of hands-on displays, as well. It's very popular with school field trips.

My grandfather brought us there to introduce us to the Collier heritage.

"Anyway," he continued, "they had this corner where you could combine different oils and make your own soap scent. To this day, I'm shocked pine-lemon-musk never made it to market."

"Quite a combination," Chris noted.

"The word is *pungent*," Thomas replied, causing the older man to chuckle. "Grandfather said it made his eyes water. After that, it was decided I should stick to the marketing and management side of the business."

Decided? Rosalind frowned at the odd word. "But you were Maddie's age."

"There was never any question we would work for Collier's. When your family's been running a business for a couple centuries, it's more or less a given," he added.

Except that he didn't go to work for Collier's. They'd moved to Cumbria.

"My grandfather used to give this speech about how the company's history was intertwined with England's. A little over the top, but it got the point across."

"That you should be proud of your heritage," Chris said.

"Precisely." Thomas paused while he chewed the last of a cookie. "I don't think I truly appreciated what he was talking about until I had to walk in his shoes.

"Having half a dozen generations stare at you on the way to your office every morning will do that," he added with a smile.

Chris nodded, stroking his beard thoughtfully. "Must be a lot of pressure trying to live up to all those expectations," he said.

"It is, but there's something very satisfying about knowing you're keeping tradition alive. Or trying to."

There was no mistaking the pride in his voice or the passion. Rosalind could see both in the way his eyes brightened, as well. And tension. Like before, there was an undercurrent to his reference to the future. The stress of expectations Chris just mentioned? She shifted in her seat. This entire conversation was leaving her with an uneasy feeling. She was ashamed to say she hadn't realized how deep Thomas's ties to the company ran. Or maybe she did realize prior to the accident, but the discomfort nagging her felt as though she hadn't truly appreciated it.

"Makes me sorry I didn't remember that story," she said out loud.

"You wouldn't have," Thomas replied. "I never told you."

Really? Why not? She tried not to frown in front of their guest.

"Can I make soap smell too, Daddy?"

"You want to make soap?" Grabbing Maddie by the waist, Thomas scooped her on to his lap. "Tell you what. When you're a little bit older, I'll take you to the museum and you can make smelly soap."

"How much older?" Maddie asked.

"Seven. Same age as I was when I went. If it's all right with your mother," he said.

Rosalind resisted the urge to squirm under all three sets of eyes. Why did she suddenly feel like the bad guy? "Two years is a long way off. Shouldn't we be focused on something that's happening sooner, like Christmas?"

With that, the conversation shifted to the festive season and the Christmas present Chris planned to buy for Jessica while he was in London.

Still, despite the change in topic, Rosalind couldn't shake the disquiet left by Thomas's story. Silly that a childhood memory would unsettle her. Her automatic instinct was to chalk it up to jealousy since her current mental state left her childhood slate blank. But it was more than jealousy. It was that Thomas revealed a piece of himself that she hadn't known.

"Oh, my, will you look at how late it's getting?" Chris exclaimed. Two hours had disappeared along with the tea and two servings of cookies. "If I'm going to get those gourmet salts for Jessica, I'd better hurry. It was good to see you again, Thomas."

"It was good to see you again, Chris."

The two men rose and shook hands before Chris bent down to look Maddie in the eye. "And you, Miss Madeline. It's safe to say you've been a very good girl. I have no doubt your friend Bigsby will get that companion he's been wanting."

Maddie beamed. "This is for you," she said.

It was the piece of paper she'd been holding when she came from the kitchen. "I made it while Daddy was making tea. He helped me with the spelling."

Curious, Rosalind peered over and saw the words "Thank you" scrawled in messy red letters.

"For letting Mummy come home for Christmas early and letting her stay."

Rosalind's heart squeezed as she looked from the note to her daughter to Chris. The older man's eyes glistened with the same emotion. "You're most welcome, Miss Madeline," he told her. "It was my pleasure."

"How about me?" Rosalind asked. She was struggling to keep the moment light. This good-bye seemed harder than the last one. "Am I on the good list?"

"Absolutely." He crushed her with his embrace, allowing her a farewell whiff of peppermint and pine. "You've got a second chance with your family this Christmas," he whispered before kissing her cheek. "You can't get better than that."

CHAPTER TEN

"DID YOU REALLY never tell me about your grandfather and all that?" Rosalind asked once Chris had departed. "Why not?"

"Never came up in conversation," he replied.

"Never? Surely we talked about our childhoods." Hadn't he implied as much the other day? "In fact, you said you envied my family's closeness."

"I did. From everything you described, the three of you were very close."

Nodding to herself, Rosalind walked over to the giant Christmas tree.

Since Thomas's comment, she'd been trying extra hard to remember the wonderful family unit he'd described. Bits and bobs had come to her. She'd remembered her father's sweaters always smelled of cloves, and of hiking in the woods. While each memory filled her with comfort, the recollections themselves were infused with significance, as though they were gifts to be treasured. She supposed they were, since she had only a handful of recollections in her head to draw upon.

Footsteps sounded and Thomas's figure appeared to her right. Immediately, awareness rippled through her. Was she ever going to be able to stand close to him and not have a physical reaction?

"Your family shared a legacy. I would think that made you close," she said.

"A different kind of closeness. Once you got outside the world of soap, the ties got a bit tenuous."

"Is that why you didn't go to work for your father after university?"

"Not at all."

"But you said yourself, you were raised to be part of the company."

"I thought it was obvious?" He poked a set of crystal bells, making them tinkle. "We haven't gone on our shopping expedition yet, you know."

"Shopping?" The comment very nearly sailed over her head; she was still stuck on the story he'd shared with Chris.

"For Maddie's Christmas presents. Now that

Santa's told her she was on the nice list, the pressure is on to make sure Bigsby gets a BFF." He poked a different set of bells. The tree was covered with bells of various sizes. This set had a lower tone. "You're still willing to shop for her presents together?"

Like on a date. She remembered. "Of course," she replied. This was about Maddie. "When would you like to go?"

"Tomorrow evening?"

"Um…" Rosalind chewed the inside of her cheek. Richard had suggested he give her a tour of the university. She'd been tempted to go if for no other reason than to escape the awareness of Thomas's overwhelming presence for a few hours.

"Sure." Maddie's Christmas was more important.

Although when Thomas smiled, causing her stomach to involuntarily do a back handspring, she wondered how wise her decision had been.

The sight of his sister drumming her fingers was never good. That she was doing her drumming on his granite counter was even more bothersome.

Thomas held up his index finger while he completed his call, partly because he needed her to wait and partly to irritate her further. He balanced out his actions by moving a platter of sugar cookies to within her reach. "Two people. Seven thirty. By the window." He waited to ensure the hostess had the info correct before setting down the phone.

"Dinner plans?" Susan bit off a snowman's hat.

"Rosalind and I are going Christmas shopping. I figured that we might as well have dinner while we are out." If dinner happened to be at a romantic restaurant, well, he could hardly be blamed for the ambiance, could he?

There was still plenty of time before Christmas. He wasn't letting her walk away from their marriage without a fight.

"Is this part of your grand plan to sweep her off her feet before she remembers the two of you were separating?"

"May have been separating," Thomas quickly corrected. "She'd gone away to think. And to answer your question, it's none of your business. Now, what is the problem that has you invading my kitchen in the middle of the afternoon?"

"What makes you think there's a problem?"

Thomas waved his fingers. "You only drum when you're irritated or you're hungry. I've given you cookies."

"And I've stopped drumming."

But she was, however, still frowning. Which meant she was unhappy about something. "Is there a personnel problem I should know about?"

"Actually, I came by to do a wellness check. You haven't been to work in over a week." She took off the snowman's head and half his midsection before continuing. "Linus and I were afraid you'd died," she said with her mouth full.

"Very funny. I didn't realize my taking a few days off was such an oddity."

"Isn't it? The last time you took a break from the company it was for three years. We were afraid you might have decided to ditch us for the country again."

Ah, so that's what brought her to his kitchen. "You talked to Linus."

"Are you seriously planning to step down from the company?"

Thomas's shoulders grew stiff. He wasn't going to have this conversation. His focus was on convincing Rosalind to stay. "Eventually. Once we launch the spa line and I'm certain the company is stable again."

"The company is stable because you're in charge. You can't leave. Without you we'd still be sorting through the mess Dad made of things. And who is supposed to fill your shoes when you leave? There isn't anyone else in the family qualified to take over. Linus sure as hell won't leave his lab."

"How about you?"

She blinked. "Did you not pay attention when we were growing up? I'm Dad in a skirt. Worse, I'm my mother and Dad in a skirt. Besides, you love running the company. You were meant to run it."

Thomas sighed and reached for a cookie. Thing was, Susan was right. He did love running the company. All those speeches his grandfather had given turned out to mean something when he finally stepped into the head office.

But he also loved his wife.

"Susan, you and everyone else knew when I agreed to help out that it was temporary."

"Because she didn't want to be here."

Wow. For a person with a psychology background, his sister could be incredibly stubborn when it came to a grudge. "You can't hold it against Rosalind for preferring a different lifestyle. I'm the one who told her the move would be temporary and then dragged it out for almost two years."

"She didn't seem to have a problem with you sucking it up while she pursued her research."

"You forget I chose to suck it up." Because Rosalind was happy. And making Rosalind happy used to be enough to make him happy.

Was enough, he corrected.

Susan had gone back to drumming her fingers. He slid the cookies closer, but she didn't take the bait. "Monomania," she said, pushing the tray back.

"Okay," Thomas replied. Whatever that meant.

"It's the obsessive pursuit of a goal to the exclusion of everything else," Susan said. "Linus thinks that's your problem. Actually, he thinks it's a Collier problem." Apparently, Linus was sharing his theory with everyone. "Either way, I think he's wrong."

"No doubt you have your own theory, Dr Collier," Thomas replied.

"It's not that complicated. You're willing to sacrifice everything for a woman who isn't willing to return the favor. Did she even know how bad things were when you took over? Why you were working like a madman?"

"I told her my father had let business slide the last few years."

"In other words, no." She rolled her eyes. "Let me guess, you're not going to tell her now either."

"What would be the point?" It wouldn't change what happened. "I'm far more interested in fixing the future."

His sister pushed away from the island with a loud sigh. "You disagree," he said as she walked away.

"With you playing the villain while she doesn't have to take responsibility for her actions? Hell, yes, I disagree," she said.

He matched her sigh with one of his own. How many times did he have to repeat himself? "First of all, Rosalind doesn't remember her actions," he said. "Second, even if she did remember, it wouldn't change my role. I neglected my wife and daughter."

"Which she made known every chance she got, or have you forgotten how frostily she treated you last spring?"

"She was unhappy." Not to mention that Sinclair was around feeding the fire.

"You're unbelievable," Susan said. "Why does everything have to fall on your shoulders? Shouldn't she have to contribute, as well?"

"When the problems are my fault..."

"That's exactly my point. The problems aren't all your fault!" She leaned against the stove where she'd gone to turn on the kettle. "I love you, Thomas, but honest to God, it drives me crazy the way you treat her like she's this faultless angel."

"Thomas?"

The two of them turned to find Rosalind standing in the kitchen doorway. Dressed in a winter-white sweater and jeans, she looked like a flawless angel. Surely that should answer his sister's question.

"Am I interrupting something?" she asked.

"Not at all. Susan stopped by to share her

thoughts on something, but I think our discussion is finished. What do you need?"

"Maddie is upstairs talking about a present she made and that you were going to help her wrap it. She was being very secretive, but apparently I'm not supposed to be involved."

"Perhaps because it's your Christmas present," Thomas replied.

"Well, she's managed to get out the wrapping paper and bows, so you might want to go upstairs before she decides to wrap all of Bigsby's friends."

"Captain Wrapping Paper to the rescue then." Looking over his shoulder, he narrowed his eyes in Susan's direction, warning her to behave. "I'll be right back."

"What was that about?" Rosalind asked once Thomas had left the room.

"What was what about?"

This was the first time she'd seen her sister-in-law since their short conversation the day of her return. She hadn't given it any thought, but while Linus had stopped by the apartment for a brief visit, Susan had stayed away.

"Thomas's comment," she said. "Sounded as though he was upset."

Susan shrugged. "Difference of opinion."

Noticing the kettle was on, Rosalind walked over to the counter to retrieve a pair of mugs from the mug tree. The air had a definite chill. Odd, but she couldn't tell if it was from December weather or the woman standing nearby. Rosalind heard a tapping noise and realized it was Susan drumming her fingertips against the glass oven front. She was staring at the floor deep in thought, her round face marred by a frown.

"Almost done your Christmas shopping?" she asked, hoping to break the ice.

"Not really. There's always something I need to buy at the last minute."

"Isn't that always the case? Thomas and I are braving the crowds tonight to get Maddie a couple of items."

"He told me. He also told me you're starting to get your memories back. You must be relieved."

"Definitely." Rosalind cradled the box of tea she was taking out of the cupboard. Just that morning while wrapping presents she'd remembered a Christmas from her childhood. "There are still a lot of blank spots, but yes. It's nice to know my brain wasn't completely wiped clean."

"The concept of dissociative fugue is a fascinating one," Susan said. "It amazes me what the brain will do to protect itself from thoughts we can't deal with. Like your accident. I wonder if we'll ever know what happened before you showed up in Lochmara."

"The doctor says I may never get those days back." They certainly weren't on the top of her list of memories to recover, regardless. "Personally, I'd much rather focus on better memories."

"Can't blame you. I'm sure Thomas would like to forget those weeks, as well. He was crushed when you went missing. Blamed himself."

"I don't think anyone's to blame," Rosalind replied. "It was an accident."

"Oh, I know. But you know Thomas. The one time he puts his interests first and it drives you off a bridge. That's how he sees things even though you and I know it takes two to tango."

"I beg your pardon?"

"When it comes to problems." Susan reached

for the kettle, which had begun to whistle. "Most issues have two sides."

"You're talking about Thomas and me." Rosalind wasn't overly surprised to hear that Thomas's sister knew about their problems; Thomas probably shared a lot with his family following the accident.

Instead of answering, Susan filled their mugs with hot water. "Did Thomas tell you why he's running Collier's?" she asked.

"He told me some. I know your father had a stroke, and we came back temporarily to help out. Then your father passed away."

"Leaving behind a royal mess. His last few years he very nearly ran the company into the ground. Linus and I aren't involved in the financial side so we had no idea, but if Thomas hadn't taken the reins, there wouldn't be a Collier's Soap Company."

"I didn't realize." Watching the amber trails seeping from the tea bag into her cup, she tried to recall the various memories she had of Thomas and his work. All she could conjure up were arguments about long hours and resentment.

"Our customer base was dying out. Literally. He reorganized the company and ordered a complete rebranding. This spa thing is his brainchild. If it works, it'll bring in the younger and high-end customers we need to keep the brand afloat."

No wonder Thomas's smile had wavered when he'd joked about the line's failure being on his head. It wasn't a joke. "I had no idea he was under such pressure."

"Probably because he never told you."

Rosalind stared at the other woman. "What? Why wouldn't he tell me?" Wasn't that something a wife should know?

"I'm not sure," Susan replied, "although I have a theory. May I be blunt?"

She wasn't being blunt already? "Yes, of course." Seeing how Thomas's workaholism was the crux of their problems, Rosalind wanted to know.

Susan crossed her arms. Although she was shorter than Rosalind, she had the Collier ability to pin a person in place with her stare. The hairs on the back of Rosalind's neck stood on end. "I think he tried to tell you, but you were too busy throwing yourself a pity party to listen."

Talk about a verbal slap. Rosalind stepped back. Pity party?

"It was obvious you hated being in London," Susan said. "The apartment was too big. The apartment was too fancy. From the day you got here, all you did was complain and talk about going home. Would you have cared if the company was going under?"

It's just soap, Thomas.

Rosalind could hear herself in her head. Was it true? Had she shut her eyes and ears to what Thomas was going through?

Or was Susan simply angry and defensive on her brother's behalf?

Carefully, she lifted her mug. "I appreciate your candor," she said over the rim.

"No, you don't," Susan replied. "No one does." She reached for her tea, started to drink and changed her mind. "Look, I know you love my brother."

Rosalind cringed. She hadn't worked out any of her feelings; they remained tangled with too many blank spots. Every time she thought she took a step toward understanding, a new memory or new piece of information held her back.

Like now.

"That's why," Susan was saying, "I thought you should know the entire picture."

In the most passive-aggressive way, of course. "No offense," Rosalind said, "but don't you think that if Thomas felt he was being unfairly judged, he'd say something rather than rely on his sister to speak on his behalf?"

"You would think so," she replied. "Unfortunately, when it comes to you, my big brother tends to think you can do no wrong. He'd give up his soul so long as it made you happy."

"If that was true, we wouldn't be in London."

Did she say that out loud? Dear God, was that how she really felt?

Susan gave a smug smile. "I rest my case."

They went shopping for Maddie's present as scheduled, deciding on a giant stuffed bear to keep Bigsby company and a few other items. As they were walking out of the toy store, Thomas said, "I made dinner reservations."

Dinner had been part of the original plan. But that was before. "I'm not sure it's a good idea," she said.

"It's dinner, Rosalind. We both need to eat, don't we?"

Exactly. She wasn't hungry. Her talk with Susan ate at her the entire time they'd been shopping. Just when she thought she'd had everything puzzled out, Thomas's sister had decided to throw another piece into the mix.

Had she really been as horrible as Susan said? After her sister-in-law left, Rosalind had gone upstairs, stared at her reflection and wondered. The woman Susan had described sounded like a brat. That couldn't be right. Thomas would never tolerate being with a brat. It didn't fit his nature.

Neither did the picture of self-sacrifice Susan painted of him.

So, which was the truth? The workaholic with the long-suffering wife or the long-suffering businessman with the shrew?

"Can I take the silence as a yes?"

Thomas looked over at her, eyes sparkling like Christmas lights.

Hard to think straight when the man could distract her with the simplest of looks. "Sure," she sighed. "Like you said, we have to eat."

"I think you'll like the place. It's keeping with the theme. Plus…" He shoved his hands in his pockets. Unlike last time, Rosalind wasn't holding his arm. "There's something I wanted to talk to you about."

"If this is about asking me to stick around past the New Year…"

"Should I?" Thomas asked. "Ask you?"

Yes.

No.

Maybe.

"You said you wanted space," Thomas continued. "I'm going to respect your request. Do I want you to stay? Absolutely. But I also know that words and promises without substance don't mean anything."

"No, they don't." His respectful acquiescence made her uncomfortable. Shouldn't he be fighting a little harder for her to stay?

Listen to yourself: leave me alone but beg me to stay. Maybe Susan was right about her and she was a shrew. Actually, she sounded like a far worse word.

They walked past Trafalgar Square. Seeing the Christmas tree reminded her of Thomas's comments about respecting history. She tried to imagine what it must be like for him to walk past his ancestors day after day. Did he feel their expectations on his shoulders? Had she ever bothered to ask?

"Was Collier's really on the verge of failing when we moved back to London?"

Her question caught him off guard and his steps stuttered. "Why do you ask?"

"Something Susan said this afternoon."

"Susan can be a pill. What did she say?"

"Actually, I'm glad she said something. When you talked about protecting Maddie's legacy, I thought it was…talk. I didn't realize that you were literally trying to save the company."

Thomas gave a sigh. "I told you, my father made some pretty bad decisions. The company was in dire straits."

Leaving it up to him to bring it back from the brink of ruin. Susan was telling the truth. "There's so much I don't know, especially about the past couple years, that I should. Susan told me that was why you were working so much. I wish I'd known."

"Why?" He stopped, his long silhouette dwarfed by the bronze lion statue behind him. "Would knowing have made you less angry?"

Susan had asked the same question. "I don't

know. Maybe." The idea that the answer might be no made her stomach churn with guilt.

"That's why Susan shouldn't have said anything."

"Don't be too mad at her," Rosalind said. "She's your sister."

"Half sister," he corrected, although she suspected it was a term he used only when annoyed with her. "Suppose I should be grateful she's only a busybody and not a loon like her mother. For once, our father's failure to focus on his wife's happiness worked in our favor. Got Susan's mother out of our lives."

Rosalind didn't comment. Something about his comment picked at her nerves.

He'd picked a rooftop restaurant. She should have known. High atop one of London's tallest buildings, the restaurant had a huge outdoor garden. Nestled among the potted Christmas trees and strings of lights were a series of glass enclosures—private igloos where couples could dine under the winter stars in warmth and comfort.

"I said I wouldn't argue with you," Thomas said as the maître d' led them to their table. "I never said I was going to turn off the charm."

God, but he was trying so hard.

"Besides, this way we can have privacy while we talk."

"There are lots of places we could have privacy." Places that weren't quite such close quarters. Or impossibly romantic.

"But none of them have a view of the Thames. I know," he said when she sighed. "One evening doesn't change anything."

"The problems we had before my accident haven't gone away, Thomas." No matter how natural it felt to sit under the stars together. "We can't snap our fingers and erase them."

"Ah, but maybe we could."

A nice dream, but unrealistic. "How? Make Collier's disappear and go back to the country?"

Thomas slipped into the seat next to hers. "That's what I wanted to talk to you about. What if I did? Make Collier's disappear."

"Are you offering to step down from your company?"

"If it meant making you happy."

Turning, he took her hands in his. "Look, I know that right now, you're struggling to remember your feelings for me. The least I can do is prove that the man you do remember has changed. If that means my leaving Collier's, then that's what I'll do."

Rosalind couldn't believe what she was hearing.

"What about Maddie's legacy?" All the history and heritage he believed so deeply in?

"There's no rule that the company has to be run by a Collier. The company will still be family owned. I'll find someone who I trust to respect the strategic plan I've put in place so that when Maddie gets older, Collier's will be there for her."

"I—I don't know what to say." Stunned, she broke from Thomas's grasp. "You would do that for me? Walk away from your family's company? From a job you love?" For a second time.

"I'd rather have a wife than a company." Gently, he took her face in his hands. Meeting his gaze, Rosalind saw a sheen in Thomas's eyes that squeezed at her heart. "We've been given a second chance, Rosie. All I want to do is make you happy."

He kissed her.

"What do you say, Rosie?" he whispered

against her lips. "Shall we go back to where we started?"

Before she could say a word, he was kissing her again, taking her silence for acceptance. Rosalind's eyes fluttered shut.

All I want is to make you happy, he'd said. From everything she remembered, going home was exactly what she'd been wanting.

So why did her stomach feel like lead?

CHAPTER ELEVEN

ALL I WANT is to make you happy.

The damn phrase refused to leave her head. It kept her from enjoying her dinner. Every time Thomas smiled at her, her stomach twisted in a knot. She was getting what she wanted, but the victory—if that's what you could call it— felt wrong.

Once again, she was missing a piece of the story.

The next day she called Richard to apologize again for canceling their plans. His modulated tones were a little more clipped than usual. "I thought for sure I'd get a call telling me he'd stood you up," he said.

"Actually, he's been around every day since… the last time he got called into the office."

"Good for him."

"Seriously." Richard probably didn't mean to sound condescending. "I think he's making a real effort."

"Perhaps you're right. The real test will be if he can continue the effort or fall off the wagon once he's won you back."

Rosalind looked down at the carpet. She was sitting in the library by the Christmas tree while Thomas and Maddie were in the other room. The easy thing would be to tell Richard that Thomas planned to give up his job, thus ending his comments. So why couldn't she?

"I only called to apologize for canceling," she said instead.

"You can make it up to me by having drinks tonight. What do you say?"

"Not tonight," she replied, rubbing her neck. The offer didn't strike her as comfortably as it should. "I'm afraid I don't want to spend two nights in a row away from Maddie. She's still getting over her fear that I might disappear again."

"Next week, then?"

"Maybe." She rubbed her neck again. Nothing Richard was saying was wrong, but her body was reacting anyway. "Next week is awfully close to Christmas."

"That's the point. We need to have a Christmas toast to your safe return. I've missed you, Rosalind. I was hoping we could…"

Could what? An image flashed into her head. A corner café. Maddie coloring on a menu.

None of this would be a problem if you'd run away with me…

Dear God, what had she done?

"Rosalind? Are you there?" Richard's voice sounded in her ear.

"S-sorry, I…" She squeezed her eyes shut, but the image had taken hold.

We could be on a flight by Friday.

The memory widened. She'd removed Richard's hand. Thank goodness. How would she have been able to look herself in the mirror?

"I need to go, Richard." She didn't bother with saying goodbye. She was too disgusted with herself. While nothing might have happened, the fact she'd let another man even think there was a possibility was just as horrifying.

Her head hurt. She needed to lie down and think about what she was going to do. About Thomas. About her memories.

As she headed toward her room, she heard voices—a voice, really—coming from Maddie's bedroom. It was Thomas. He looked ridiculous with his tall frame folded in a chair at Maddie's play table. His phone was tucked under one ear, while he separated cotton balls for whatever art project he and Maddie were doing.

"You tell Ming that he's got as deep a discount as he's going to get," he was saying. "If he balks, pull the deal. I don't care how many spas he owns, we won't be bullied."

He continued for a few more minutes, confidently rattling off production numbers and percentages from the top of his head while at the same time entertaining Maddie by making faces.

Rosalind watched from the doorframe and felt her heart opening. "Very impressive," she said when he ended his call. "You're very good at that." It was the same compliment she'd offered during their flight home, when she was seeing him through a stranger's eyes.

Finished with the cotton balls, Thomas pushed the pile closer to Maddie before handing the girl a glue stick. "Which one?" he asked Rosalind. He grinned over his shoulder. "Barking about subcontractors or separating cotton balls?"

"We're making Santa a picture," Maddie volunteered. "The cotton's for his beard."

"I'm sure he'll appreciate the effort, and the answer is both," she said. "You're good at both." Every time he looked at Maddie, she could see the love etched in his face.

For that matter, Rosalind saw it whenever he looked at her.

Thomas loved fiercely. Always had. The realization came from her heart, not her head.

And it made her feel awful.

Little by little the picture of her behavior these past eighteen months was becoming clear, and, frankly, it wasn't attractive. Amnesia gave her an objectivity that hadn't been there six months ago. What she saw was a woman who, like a child, had turned her displeasure over their relocation into a months' long pout, demanding Thomas change and that Thomas give in to her wishes. Worse, rather than try and see Thomas's point of view, she'd allowed Richard Sinclair to fuel her bitterness and widen the gap between them.

It hadn't been fair of her. Hadn't been fair at all.

"You can't leave Collier's," she said,

Not surprisingly, Thomas looked at her like she had ten heads. "What are you talking about? We agreed last night."

Actually, they hadn't agreed on anything. Thomas had offered, and she... She'd lost her mind in a fog of his kisses. "Collier's needs you," she said. "It never dawned on me until just now, but you were meant to run Collier's Soap." As his grandfather and father had intended.

Pulling away from the molding, she stood upright with her arms hugging her midsection. "I wouldn't be able to live with myself knowing you'd walked away from your purpose solely to please me."

"There's no better reason, as far as I'm concerned."

Rosalind had no doubt he meant every word. The gleam that flashed in his eyes said so. "It's not right," she said. "You need to stay."

Thomas unfolded himself from the child's chair. He looked over his shoulder to make sure Maddie was distracted before closing the distance between them. "Does that mean you've changed your mind about staying in London?" he asked.

This time the gleam was more than a flash.

"I…" How was she supposed to answer? She still hated the city. In fact, the more her memory improved, the more she disliked the crowds and noise. She wanted to raise her daughter the way she'd been raised. In a small village where there was green and hills.

She looked away. "No," she said. As much as Thomas belonged here at Collier's, she belonged elsewhere.

"I see." His shoulders sagged, her stomach sagging with them. "Where then does that lead us?"

Where indeed? Much as she hated to admit it, they'd come full circle, to the place they'd been six months earlier.

"I think I need some space," she said.

CHAPTER TWELVE

I NEED SOME SPACE.

This couldn't be happening. Not again.

Thomas grabbed the doorframe, his nails digging into the wood. He was trying his best to look composed while inside he was shattering. Surely he'd heard wrong.

Last night, they'd been on the same page—or so he'd thought. "What happened?"

"Nothing happened." Turning away, she crossed the hall to the iron railing where she stood looking down on the living room. "That's the problem. We're back where we were six months ago."

"No, we're not," Thomas replied. "Six months ago I hadn't decided to walk away from Collier's."

"Which I've already said I don't want you doing. It's not right. Your company needs you."

"Susan said something to you?" Saying how

much the company needed him was something his sister would do.

"Susan has nothing to do with this."

"Then… Richard." Someone else who liked to stir the drama and keep the two of them at odds. "He said something."

Her shoulders immediately stiffened. "What does he have to do with anything?"

Thomas didn't know, but the little busybody meant something. Her rigid posture said so.

"Can't you see that we're at an impasse? I don't want to live in London and you…"

"Said I would move."

"But you don't want to," she said, turning back around. Seeing the resignation mixed with the dampness in her eyes killed him. She was giving up the fight. Giving up on them.

"Don't you see?" she said. "All we would be doing is trading one person's unhappiness for another's. It's not right."

"I wouldn't be unhappy." Not really. Not completely. He would find…something. He did before.

"Yes, you would. You're giving up your legacy."

"So I'll work from home."

"Run a company from hours away?"

"Why not? Linus is always telling me I need to work on finding shades of gray. I could divide my time."

"Sure, and then before we realize, the two of us will be arguing over how much time you spend away from home." She shook her head. "I don't think so."

"So…this is it? You're going to walk away without trying to find a solution?" There was more going on. Thomas could sense it. Feel it hovering in the air between them. But what? What'd happened between last night and now that changed her mind? "Without giving me any kind of explanation?"

"I just gave you an explanation," she replied.

"No, what you did was run a scenario through your head and make a decision. That's not an explanation."

"What more do you want me to say?"

"You could…"

Thomas rammed his fingers through his hair, frustration mounting. For the past eighteen months he'd been fighting a battle where the rules kept shifting and no matter what he did, he was wrong. Save the company. Save his marriage. Go to London. Leave London. Stay in London. Mourn his wife. Reconnect with his wife. Lose his wife. It was all too much to keep track of. Every time he took a step in one direction, he was asked to turn around and choose another.

"Just tell me what I'm supposed to do, dammit."

"I don't…"

"To win you back. To save our marriage. To make things right. Anything." He was tired of trying to trying to read minds. "I'm trying, Rosie, but I can't do all the work alone."

"I know," she replied. Tears shone in her eyes. "I know, and it's unfair."

As he watched one break free and run down her cheek, Thomas kicked himself.

"That's another reason I need the break," she said, wiping the tear away. "I need to think. About us."

It was six months ago, all over again. Despite fearing the answer, he had to ask. He had to know where he stood. If he stood anywhere at all. "Do you even want to try?"

Taking a deep breath, she closed her eyes, preventing him from seeing the emotion in their depths. An answer in itself, really. "I have some things I need to work out. Memories…"

He didn't need to hear anymore. Fists clenched against the pain tearing through him, Thomas focused on the one thing that mattered. "What about Maddie? We were supposed to be giving her a family Christmas. Are you planning to cut me out of that too?"

"What? No. Never." She lifted her hand toward him, only to change her mind and pull back. "We'll be back for Christmas Eve. I'm only taking her now because I don't think she could handle our being separated again. Her and me."

"But I can."

"I didn't mean—"

"Don't." There wasn't an argument she could make. Plus, she was right. Maddie needed her. Whether Thomas did too was inconsequential at this point.

"Just be back by Christmas Eve. That's all I ask."

"You have my word."

Like he had had her word that June's trip was going to be only for a few days? Apples and oranges, he knew, but he feared the outcome would be the same.

Suddenly, he felt very, very tired. Too tired to fight the inevitable. "I have some phone calls to make. I'll be in the library."

"Thomas."

Her call stopped him.

"I meant it earlier. You can't resign. You're too good at what you do. Collier's needs you."

At least someone did.

She'd told Maddie they were going to Cumbria to have a mummy-daughter adventure. In reality she'd picked Cumbria because it was where everything began. Both for her and Thomas, and for her before that. She'd hoped the cottage might spur on more memories and help her process her thoughts.

The cottage wasn't fancy. She knew it wouldn't be. A simple two-bedroom building with a living room and a dated kitchen.

There was a fireplace though and, two nights into the visit, she stood, cradling a cup of hot chocolate and watching the flames as they crackled and popped. Earlier in the day, she and Maddie had decorated the mantle with evergreen branches they cut from the back-yard. Same way Rosalind and her mother did when she was a little girl, she realized. For an added bit of festive whimsy, they'd hung heavy woolen socks on the nails. Three, because Mad-die insisted Thomas needed one too.

A tiny tree sat in the corner as well, strung with popcorn and paper snowflakes. Compen-sation for the trees they left behind.

All and all, it was a sweet setting, exactly the setting that had flashed through her brain in bits and pieces, and about as far removed from the London house as you could get. Weight pressed on her shoulders as she sipped her hot cocoa. You'd think, after all her discomfort in London, these surroundings would relax her, but she felt as uncomfortable as ever.

Since arriving, more and more memories had come rushing back. Some were of her child-hood, the images from photographs she'd stud-ied growing details. Like the time her parents returned home from a conference in Switzer-land and, declaring a personal holiday, whisked her away from school to come here for a week-end full of camping.

What about my legacy? she'd tossed at Thomas

during one of their arguments. She'd been talking about this cottage. The place where her family went to be a family when her parents weren't in the field or lecturing on their findings.

Now though, most of her memories were about recent events. Like sitting at the kitchen table studying samples while Thomas stood by the window, a bright red dish towel slung over his broad shoulder. There was a very ornate, very expensive cradle in the spare room in which she remembered placing Maddie down to sleep.

A gift from Linus, she realized, the memory hitting. They hadn't exactly been cut off from Thomas's family while out here, had they? Nor had she gone to London not knowing the world she was entering.

Truth was every time a memory struck she felt more and more ashamed. The other afternoon, when Thomas pressed her for an explanation as to why she was leaving, she couldn't tell him the truth: she wasn't sure she deserved a reconciliation. Here was Thomas, ready to give up everything—again—while she…

Because there's so much call for geologists in London.

She'd wallowed like a child. Pouting when her research project got canceled. Demanding they move back to her childhood home. So wrapped in self-pity had she been that she couldn't see— hadn't seen—the pressure Thomas was under. Instead, she'd turned him into the villain. Laid everything at his feet rather than tried to see the situation from his point of view.

And Richard… Her stomach lurched with disgust. What right did she have to ask Thomas to give up anything?

God, she missed him though. In just a couple weeks he'd become an integral part of her. Her present, not her past. She and Maddie would be busy doing something and her mind would drift to what Thomas might be doing. Was he hurting over what she'd said? Was he working himself too hard?

She missed his laugh. His smell. The sound of his voice.

And then the guilt would hit her once more.

Looking to her lap, she eyed the phone Thomas had given her. Time to pay the piper. She snatched up the phone and hit Autodial before she could lose her nerve.

"This is a surprise. After the last time we

spoke I didn't think I'd hear from you for quite a while." Richard's normally melodic voice sounded petulant and clipped.

Rosalind rested her mug on her thigh. Her legs were twitching, making the liquid slosh against the sides. "I'm sorry about the other night," she said.

"You hung up on me and didn't call back for three days."

"I know. Something came to me that I needed to process. I, um, may I ask you a question?"

"A quick one. I'm heading to a friend's party. Where are you anyway? The reception is awful."

"Cumbria. I came up to the cabin to think."

"Again."

"Yes, again." Glancing around her, Rosalind saw herself pacing the floors in June. She'd come to a decision…

"What was your question?" Richard asked. A closet door opened in the background.

"I need to know if… That is, did we…?" She took a deep breath. Best way to do this was to ask all at once. "I keep having this memory of you putting your hand on my knee."

There was a pause, then Richard's deep laugh

floated through the receiver. "And you think something was going on between the two of us?"

"Was there?"

"Seriously?" He laughed again. "You're too funny."

"This isn't a joke, Richard." Gripping onto the phone, she glared at his invisible expression, which judging from his earlier laugh was probably a smile.

"Of course it isn't," he replied. "But then, it is. You and me... Sweetheart, I'm gay!"

What?

"But that day at lunch in Canary Wharf. You said we should run away together."

"On a geo-archeological adventure, not as a couple."

We'll go to Angkor and find the road to Battambang.

Oh, God. She remembered now. The mythical road across Tonle Sap, one of their favorite points of discussion. Rosalind's entire body turned crimson. "I was complaining about not having a purpose and you suggested I join your expedition."

"And you told me a month in Cambodia wouldn't solve your problems…"

But that she would think about it.

"I'm an idiot."

"Yes, you are," Richard replied. "I love you, Rosalind, but you are so not my type."

Thank God. For the first time in days, she felt like she could breathe. "Then why were you always on me about Thomas? Saying I deserved better?"

"Because. That's what you wanted to hear."

Was it? "But we're friends," she said. "Shouldn't you have told me what I *needed* to hear?"

"Would you have listened?"

The words "Of course" sprang to her lips, but she bit them back. They tasted wrong.

At least, she thought as she hung up the phone, she could wipe one crime from her record. But knowing she'd misread the Richard memory didn't erase her other actions. She'd still been a stubborn child, wanting everything her way without any sort of compromise.

Funny how in forgetting what had happened, she was finally able to see the situation more clearly.

Question was, how did they solve the original problem without Thomas giving up everything or her being frustrated and miserable?

The problem with taking a good look at yourself is that there was a good chance you wouldn't like what you would see. In Rosalind's case, the more she looked at the pieces, the more she began to realize that she shared the blame for whatever problems had befallen her marriage.

Sure, Thomas worked endless hours and had in the past reneged on promises to his family. But from what Rosalind could tell, after her grant fell through she'd done nothing to improve her situation. Instead, she'd played the martyr. Insisting that Thomas give up everything so she could go back to the life she preferred. She hadn't even attempted to see circumstances from Thomas's point of view or seek some kind of compromise.

Rosalind sighed. For nearly two days she'd been pacing the entire house assessing the breakdown of her marriage with nothing to show for it but a pad full of doodles reflecting her jumbled mind. And not even current doodles at that. Most of them were from a previous visit.

The more she thought, the more she realized it was no wonder that she and Thomas had gotten to the verge of separation. They were two people unable—or unwilling—to find middle ground. Their whole marriage had been one sacrificing for the other. First Thomas, giving up his career to live in Cumbria, and then her moving to London. Although in her case, the sacrifice had been made far less willingly.

Marriage was supposed to be about working together, not surrendering yourself. Yet martyrdom was exactly what both she and Thomas had done. A person could sublimate themselves only for so long before they became bitter and angry. It was what had happened to her. It's what she feared would happen to Thomas if he carried through on his plan to leave Collier's.

So what should she do?

If the last weeks had shown her anything, it was that beneath all the stubbornness, she and Thomas had something worth saving.

She loved him.

Not the memory of him, but the man who'd

been moving heaven and earth to charm her these past few weeks.

The man who'd messed up more than once, yet in the end did everything he could to keep his promise.

The man who negotiated contracts while helping their daughter glue cotton balls on a picture of Santa Claus.

That kind, earnest man, so desperate to do right by his family.

Now it was time for her to do right by Thomas, but how? She didn't dare go back to him without some kind of handle on the changes she was going to make in order to give their marriage a fighting chance.

Sighing, she stared at the doodles in front of her, hoping for some kind of inspiration. Unfortunately, one couldn't find much inspiration from a bunch of scribbles. She'd be better off...

Rosalind blinked. Turned the paper forty-five degrees and blinked again.

Turned out the answer had been staring her right in the face the whole time.

"Call her. You know you want to."

His eyes glued on the behemoth Christmas

tree, Thomas shook his head. "I promised to give her space."

He heard the sound of footsteps as Linus came up to stand beside him. The two were in the living room because it was the only room besides the spare bedroom that Thomas could stand being in. The only room besides the spare bedroom that didn't have memories of Rosalind attached. Current memories, that is. Lucky him, he got to deal with two sets.

"It's been a week," his brother said. "How much more space does she need?"

"Tomorrow's Christmas Eve. She'll be back then." If there was one thing he was certain of, it was that Rosalind would want to give Maddie a family Christmas like they'd promised. He ignored the anxious voice pointing out that he'd been certain she'd return in June too.

"And you're still planning to quit?" Linus asked.

"I am." His resignation notice was typed and ready to be distributed to the company. As of the end of January, he would no longer be Collier's president. He boxed in his sadness about departing with his anxiety. He'd walked away from his legacy before and survived. Life would go on again. What was a legacy anyway if he didn't have someone with whom he could share it?

"Didn't you tell me Rosalind asked you to stay?"

"That was her guilty conscience talking," he replied. "She was asking for space and didn't want me prematurely giving up anything."

A third voice he needed to ignore suggested her guilty conscience was over knowing she planned to leave for good. The box in the back of his mind was getting very crowded.

"When push comes to shove, though, whether I give up Collier's is my choice." An easy one to make too. He poked at one of the silver balls that dangled from the tree's branches, making it sway. "I'd cut off my own arm if it meant saving my marriage."

"Surprised you haven't."

"What?" He whipped his head around. Linus's remark had a distinctly derisive drawl. "What are you suggesting?"

"Nothing," Linus replied. "Only that it's painfully obvious that you'd sacrifice anything for Rosalind. You always have."

"Of course. It's called making a marriage

work, Linus. I know it's a foreign concept in this family, but sometimes you have to put your partner's needs before your own."

"You know what else is a foreign concept? Compromise. I need a drink. You want one?"

Again, Thomas shook his head. "Alcohol will only make me maudlin."

"More maudlin. You've been maudlin for days."

"Can you blame me?"

"Didn't say I did."

Mrs Faison had arranged glasses and several bottles of spirits on the credenza in anticipation of holiday entertaining. Not that Thomas had been in any kind of entertaining mood. He turned his back on the tree and watched as Linus studied the different labels.

"For your information, I compromise." He knew where his brother was trying to go with the remark. "I am more than capable of seeing shades of gray in a situation."

"In business, maybe. When it comes to your marriage..." Shrugging, he unscrewed the cap on a bottle and sniffed. "I think you'd rather cut off your arm."

Thomas changed his mind about the drink.

Crossing the space, he started dropping ice cubes, loudly, into a glass.

"I'm not sure I like what you're implying." His brother made it sound like he was being some kind of martyr. "Not to mention that you're completely wrong."

"Am I?"

"I wasn't exactly amputating any limbs the last eighteen months, was I?" In fact, maybe if he had, he wouldn't be in this situation.

"Instead, Collier's would be in receivership and you'd be pretending to enjoy being a country carpenter."

Thomas hadn't realized he'd spoken aloud and resented Linus's comeback. He glowered while Linus filled both their glasses to the halfway mark with gin.

"Well, aren't you quite the expert this evening? I didn't realize we had a clairvoyant in the family." How did he know what Thomas enjoyed and didn't enjoy?

"Are you telling me you enjoyed what you were doing?"

"Of course I did."

"As much as you enjoy running Collier's?"

"Apples and oranges. You can't compare the

two." There was a meaning attached to Collier's that didn't exist with carpentry—or any other job for that matter. And carpentry didn't come with the same kind of excitement or rush of satisfaction that he felt when the business was clicking on all cylinders. They weren't the same kind of fires. The stakes weren't the same.

All right, so maybe he didn't love being a carpenter. What did that matter? "My wife wasn't miserable when I was a carpenter."

"Rosalind was definitely miserable here. That's for sure."

"Yes," Thomas replied, snatching the bottle of tonic from Linus's hand. "Because of me."

Letting out a long sigh, Linus set his glass down. "You know, I'm beginning to think Susan was right. Subtle isn't the answer."

"Don't even mention Susan. I haven't forgiven her for whatever it is she said to Rosalind the other day."

"Probably the truth. Although knowing Susan, she was a little too blunt." Taking back the tonic water, he began to pour. "Remember the other day when I shared my theory about the Collier curse? That the Colliers lacked a moderation gene? I was wrong."

"I could have told you that."

"Says the man who coined the phrase 'Collier curse.' The three of us do suffer from an inability to see beyond black and white, but that's not where I went wrong. My mistake was thinking you'd pick up on the hint about your behavior. *You're* the one with tunnel vision. You seem to think you can have either Collier's or marriage but not both."

"You don't know what you're talking about." Thomas turned back to the Christmas tree. None of this talk had anything to do with his marriage or his decision to leave Collier's. Linus and Susan had never been married. Who were they to pass judgment?

"Maybe I don't," Linus said. "But I am a scientist by nature, and as a result I do a lot of observing. And over the last five—no, seven years—I've watched you act as though there were only two choices. People balance marriage and career all the time."

"Not in our family," Thomas replied.

"Grandfather had an ego the size of the British Empire. And Preston…he married Susan's mother. Doesn't that say enough?"

He returned to his spot by Thomas's shoulder.

"All I'm saying is that there might have been more at play than their dedication to Collier's. You just weren't looking at the whole picture.

"Same way you might not be seeing the past couple of years as accurately as you should," he added, clapping a hand on Thomas's shoulder. "The truth bomb our Susan tossed at Rosalind the other day? She let her know Rosalind wasn't so innocent in the whole debacle as you were leading her to believe."

Thomas shrugged away from his touch. "What are you talking about? Of course Rosalind's innocent."

"I think your guilt over the accident gave you amnesia too, Thommy-boy. Have you forgotten how much complaining Rosalind did?"

"Of course she complained. I asked her to give up her life, and then practically ignored her."

"Really? I seem to remember you trying to appease her. Granted, you didn't do too good a job…"

I'm trying the best I can, Rosie.

It was an argument he'd given over and over. He was trying his best, but there were thousands of jobs and two hundred years to save.

And God help him, he enjoyed it. For all the headaches and stress, he enjoyed the job.

That was the biggest part of his guilt. If he'd enjoyed his job less, he might have saved his marriage and saved Rosalind six months of missing time.

His shoulders sagged. "Doesn't matter." What mattered was having Rosalind in his life. Having his family together. He was nothing without her. "I have to save my marriage."

"No one is telling you not to, Thommy-boy. All I'm saying is that it took two to create the problem. Maybe it should take two of you to create the solution."

CHAPTER THIRTEEN

HAVING TWO PEOPLE solve the problem was eas-
ier said than done, especially if one of the people wasn't there to talk.

Christmas Eve came and there was no sign
of Rosalind or Maddie. At first, he told himself
they'd gotten a late start. Maddie could be a
handful when she didn't want to cooperate. Rosalind's phone must have died, which was why
she hadn't called or responded to his texts. No
news was good news. The police called when
there was an accident; he knew from taking
the call in the past. As long as the phone didn't
ring, everything was okay.

They would be home soon.

But, as twilight fell, so did his hope. The
belief that they would be home soon became
the knowledge that maybe they were simply
staying away. Funny how the threat of aban-

donment became preferable depending on the circumstances.

He stood in the library watching the snow-flakes begin to fall, his heart in his throat. He was alone. His phone had been ringing all afternoon. Linus, Susan, a host of business calls. He'd ignored them all. If his world was going to break apart, he wanted to be alone when it happened.

Outside, the Christmas lights were coming on. Traffic was getting lighter. People were starting their festivities.

Someone on the street was ringing sleigh bells.

He squeezed his eyes shut. "Please," he whispered. "She doesn't have to stay but let them come home for Christmas."

"Daddy!"

Thomas's eyes flew open. "Maddie?" He rushed to the hallway. Sure enough, his daughter was running into the living room.

"Daddy! It's Christmas!" she was screeching. "It's Christmas!"

He practically slid down the stairs to hug her hello. "Merry Christmas, sweetheart," he whispered as he squeezed her tight. Tears of relief burned the inside of his eyelids.

"Santa brought us home and he gave me cookies," she said, wrapping her arms around his waist.

From over Maddie's head he saw Rosalind come toward him. She had snowflakes in her hair and on her jacket. When she saw his moist eyes, a hand flew to her mouth.

"I'm so sorry. I dropped my phone in a puddle and killed it," she said. "Chris tried to call a couple times but you didn't answer."

Chris?

Sure enough, Chris McKringle came stomping down the steps into the living room. "Merry Christmas!" he greeted as he shook the snow from his red knit cap. "I happened to be in Cumbria just as these two lassies were getting ready to head home. Since it was snowing, I thought it might be a good idea to follow and make sure she came home."

"I told him he didn't have to, but he insisted," Rosalind replied.

"No sense in tempting fate a second time. Especially since I wasn't sure how comfortable she'd be driving in the weather."

"Looks like we owe you yet another thank-you." Thomas let go of Maddie so he could extend his hand.

"You don't owe me a thing. Jessica would have my head if I didn't make sure our Lammie got home safe. We're mighty fond of her."

"So am I." Thomas cast Rosalind a look, only to find her eyes cast downward, hidden from view. His spirits flagged, but he tried his best to keep the worry from showing as he shook Chris's hand. "I'm sorry it's costing you Christmas with your wife though." No way he'd make it back to Lochmara until the middle of tomorrow.

"No worries there. She's used to me being out and about. We're spending the holidays with some friends a little way north of here. I'll be seeing her soon enough."

After a few minutes more of conversation, the Scotsman stuck his cap back on his head and said his goodbyes. Thomas and Rosalind walked him to the door. "Merry Christmas to you both," he said, giving Rosalind a giant hug. "Go and make the most of your Christmas Eve. It can be one of the most romantic times of the year, you know." Then, giving a wink and nod, out the door he went.

Leaving the two of them standing face-to-face.

"We need to talk," they said in unison.

Thomas held up a hand. "Sorry. You first." If he was going to hear bad news, he'd rather hear it now so he could have time to put on a good face for Maddie. He steeled himself for the news.

Rosalind took a deep breath to calm her heart. Where to start? There was so much she wanted to say. She'd spent the entire drive practicing but now that the time had come, all the words were rushing to come out at once.

"I'm sorry I worried you. I really did break my phone." She couldn't believe how it'd slipped out of her pocket straight into the one random puddle at the gas station.

"What matters is you're home now."

"I'm sorry I wasn't home sooner. I'm sorry I took so long to think things out." She paused. Carefully choosing her next words.

"I was wrong," she said. Slowly, so they would have time to resonate. "All the problems we were having, I put them all on your shoulders, and I shouldn't have. I... I remember now. I remember a lot of things. How harsh and unhappy I was because life wasn't how I wanted it, and I took that unhappiness out on you."

He shook his head. "I didn't help matters. I was never around..."

"No, you weren't." But she wasn't going to let him shoulder all the blame anymore. "But I should have talked to you more. I mean, really talked," she said when he went to disagree. "About what I was thinking and feeling. Instead, I complained and expected you to do all the work to solve my issues. I never stopped to think about the pressures you were under."

"Because I didn't talk to you either," Thomas replied. "I was afraid to admit how much Collier's meant to me or how much I liked running the company."

"I knew. I could see it in your eyes."

The revelation came one night while she'd been watching the fire. She'd remembered pieces of a dinner party and Thomas sitting at the head of the table. He had the glow of pride about him. Of command. And she remembered realizing it was from being in his element.

"And I was jealous," she said. "You'd made your whole world about me and suddenly I had to share it with your legacy."

"I swore I'd never be like my father or grandfather."

"You're not." Having confessed her fear, Rosalind felt lighter. It was as though all the months of hoarding her emotions had weighed her down.

With lightness came bravery. Only a few inches separated them, and she stepped close, cradling his cheek in her palm.

"When I think of all the times you put my needs first during our marriage…"

His hand reached out to cradle hers in return. "Not nearly enough. I should have worked harder to keep my promises."

"And I shouldn't have put so much pressure on you to be the answer to my happiness. I love you, Thomas Collier. So very, very much."

Thomas didn't say anything. He didn't have to. Instead, he kissed her. Before she could answer, he kissed her. Slowly and purposefully. A once-in-a-lifetime kiss or, in her case, maybe twice in a lifetime. The kind of kiss that spoke what words couldn't. Closing her eyes, Rosalind wrapped her arms around his neck, giving herself to the moment.

When the kiss ended, Rosalind lay her head against Thomas's lapel and listened to his heart beating against her ear.

"You know..." Thomas kissed the top of her head. "Linus says that we need to work on learning to compromise."

"Linus is a very smart man," she said. "Do you think we can?"

"I'm willing if you are. But then, I'm crazy in love with you."

Smiling, Rosalind closed her eyes and held him tight. This wasn't the end of their problems, but it was the beginning of a solution. Life had truly given them a second chance, and she intended to make sure they didn't waste the opportunity.

"Guess that makes two of us," she told him.

Six months later

"Admit it, we're lost." Thomas looked over at his wife who was wearing the cutest frown on her face as she poked at the touch screen of her phone.

"We are not lost. The GPS on my phone froze.

I'm almost positive this is the correct road though. I remember those rock formations."

"Naturally." He laughed when she reached across and swatted his arm.

They were on a second-honeymoon-slash-research trip to the Scottish Highlands and had decided to pay Chris and Jessica a surprise visit. Having not connected with the older couple since Chris had followed her home Christmas Eve, Rosalind was eager to say hello and share their good news.

They'd spent most of the winter talking and learning how to truly communicate. Much as Thomas hated to admit it, Linus had been right. It took two to solve their issues. Together they'd laid out their desires and their fears, and created a compromise. While it took some time, Thomas came to realize he could delegate tasks without Collier's falling apart. Right before the botanical line's launch, he hired hired a second in command. Someone who could deal with the day-to-day crises while he focused on steering Collier's toward the future.

Meanwhile, Rosalind had realized that a large part of her issues were that she missed the stimulation of research. Turned out, she told him, that she'd discovered that part of the answer right before her accident. Two words scribbled in the corner of the notepad had jarred the memory: glacial erosion. It was why she'd gone to western Scotland. To refresh her memory on a couple of key points about the landscape. She was now happily soliciting funding for a new study on glacial erosion in the Highlands.

And they'd moved from London. Not to Cumbria, but to a house in a small town within commuting distance of London. A town that held no connection to either family and could truly become the connection to theirs.

Because it was expanding. That was the real reason for their visit to the McKringles. Thomas looked at Rosalind's midsection and grinned.

"Are you going to stare at my belly from now until Christmas?" Rosalind asked.

"Probably." Shifting gears, he rounded the corner. There were days when he thought he might burst from being so happy. "When I think of the hell I was going through a year ago, and how things are now…"

They weren't done working. Successful marriages always took work. But today, as he drove down this Scottish country road, he was happier than he'd ever imagined. He had his wife, a lovely daughter and a child due Christmas Eve. It was a miracle, that's what it was.

"There's the marker." Rosalind pointed as the sign reading Lochmara appeared a few yards ahead. "The restaurant should only be a mile or so. Around that bend in the road."

"Unless you misremembered the rock formation."

"Thomas Collier, I may have forgotten many things, but I never forget a rock. Look, there's the building."

A building, yes, but not McKringle's Pub. It was nothing but a broken-down, old icehouse.

Exchanging a look, they stepped out of the car. Most of the windows were boarded up as was the faded front door, making it impossible to look inside. Didn't matter. It was obvious that the building had been vacant for a long time.

"Hate to break it to you, my love, but it looks like your rock memory is slipping," Thomas said.

"But I could have sworn..." She was frowning again.

It was strange, he had to admit. The building looked the same. Exactly how many other back roads with icehouses could there be in this area? "Why don't we drive into the town and ask for better directions?"

He turned to lead her back to the car when he spotted something by the bottom of the door. A tiny Scottish flag had been wedged in between the door and the board. Just like the ones that had decorated McKringle's wreath.

There was a piece of paper wrapped around the staff. Thomas unrolled it. "It can't be," he muttered.

Rosalind knelt down. "What does it say?"

"You're not going to believe it."

He wasn't sure he did. Although in a weird way, maybe it made sense. A warm sense of contentment washed over him.

Leaning over, he kissed her. "Have I told you today how much I love you, Mrs Collier?"

"I love you too. Now, what does the note say?"

"The note says, 'Merry Christmas. PS: Have you considered the name Noel?'"

* * * * *

LET'S TALK
Romance

For exclusive extracts, competitions
and special offers, find us online:

f facebook.com/millsandboon

⊙ @millsandboonuk

🐦 @millsandboon

Or get in touch on 0844 844 1351*

For all the latest titles coming soon,
visit millsandboon.co.uk/nextmonth

*Calls cost 7p per minute plus your phone company's price per
minute access charge

Want even more
ROMANCE?

Join our bookclub today!

'Mills & Boon books, the perfect way to escape for an hour or so.'

Miss W. Dyer

'Excellent service, promptly delivered and very good subscription choices.'

Miss A. Pearson

'You get fantastic special offers and the chance to get books before they hit the shops'

Mrs V. Hall

**Visit millsandbook.co.uk/Bookclub
and save on brand new books.**

MILLS & BOON